THE SPIDER:
DICTATOR'S DEATH MERCHANTS

DICTATOR'S DEATH-MERCHANTS

By Grant Stockbridge

POPULAR PUBLICATIONS • 2026

PUBLISHING HISTORY

"Dictator's Death-Merchants" originally appeared in the July, 1940 (Vol. 21, No. 2) issue of *The Spider* magazine. Copyright 2026 by Argosy Communications, Inc. All rights reserved.

Visit POPULARPUBLICATIONS.COM FOR more books like this.

CHAPTER 1
RECEPTION À LA SPIDER

IT WAS on the afternoon of the twenty-third of May, that the gentleman who was known as Edouardo Estéban arrived by plane at LaGuardia Airport, in New York City.

Señor Estéban was a small man, dark complexioned, and with a constantly watchful air about him. His dark and restless eyes darted everywhere, as if in search of hidden enemies. Throughout the customs inspection, he was tense.

One of the other plane passengers had a portable radio, and when the instrument blared into sound, Señor Estéban jumped. But then he listened with strange grimness to the short news announcement: "*. . . Police Commissioner Kirkpatrick has cancelled all departmental leaves, and has assigned every available man to the task of guarding New York City's banks. The city-wide hunt for the saboteurs, who have destroyed three large banking establishments in three days, is being conducted with intensity. Commissioner Kirkpatrick has asked the War Department to check all possible sources from which the wreckers could have secured the five hundred pound demolition bombs which shattered the buildings. . . .*"

There was a buzz of conversation in the room, as the passengers began to discuss the three day terror which had struck New York, culminating in the complete destruction of the Hudson River Bank at nine o'clock the previous night. Every night at nine o'clock, another banking institution was being pulverized

NATIONAL
100
100

by high-power demolition bombs. Everybody hazarded an opinion as to the possible motives of the unknown criminal organization behind the outrages....

But Señor Estéban did not join the conversation.

As soon as they had cleared the customs, the passengers boarded the luxurious limousine bus in which they were to be taxied into New York City. Edouardo Estéban occupied the last seat in the bus, and kept looking constantly out of the window, watching every car that passed by him.

His eyes were restless and sharp, like the eyes of a bird that is poised for instant flight.

Just as the bus was passing through a deserted section of Long Island City, a motorcycle screamed up alongside, with siren wailing.

The driver, thinking it was a motorcycle cop, slowed down. He turned to look out of the window, and cursed. The motorcycle rider was not a policeman. His face was in shadow, but the gun which he pointed at the bus driver was very businesslike.

"Pull over," said the man on the motorcycle.

The muzzle of that gun was big and ugly, and the bus driver obeyed with alacrity.

The man on the motorcycle raised a whistle to his lips, and blew a single sharp blast. Out of the darkness behind, a station wagon appeared. Five men piled out of it, all armed. Their leader was a squat man with a face that looked as if it had been frozen into an expressionless mask. He was carrying a submachine gun under his arm. He climbed into the bus and stood at the head of the aisle, facing the terrified passengers. His mouth twisted into a very satisfied grin when he saw Señor Edouardo Estéban in the rear.

"Good evening, Don Estéban," he said. He swung the submachine gun forward. "Would you like to die right here, or would you prefer to come outside and take it?"

It must be said for Señor Estéban, that he did not cringe. His face was white and strained, but he arose with dignity.

"I will go outside with you, Kinley. Do not shoot here. There are ladies and children."

STOICALLY, HE marched down the aisle, while the other gunmen from the station wagon covered the passengers through the windows of the bus.

Señor Estéban descended to the ground, and Kinley followed him. He turned the muzzle of the submachine gun upon the Mexican gentleman.

"You are being executed," he said, "by the order of *El Crocodilo.* You can save your life by talking."

"What is it you wish to know?"

Kinley grinned. "You came here to contact the Spider. You are bringing information to the Spider about *El Crocodilo.* Is that correct?"

"Perhaps."

"If you'll tell us where to find the Spider, you will be allowed to live. Talk fast."

"I am sorry," said Señor Edouardo Estéban. "A true Mexican gentleman does not betray a friend. A true Mexican gentleman knows how to die." With head held high, he faced the submachine gun. "Shoot!"

Kinley gave him a twisted grin. He thrust the submachine gun forward so that the muzzle touched Estéban's chest. His finger curled around the trip.

"All right, sucker," he said. "Let's see what your friend the Spider can do for you now—"

He never finished the sentence.

Suddenly the night was filled with a loud and terrible laughter. To the ears of those gunmen, and of the passengers in the bus, it seemed as if some mighty god of the ancients had come down from the skies and was uttering brazen throated peals of doom.

As abruptly as it had begun, that strange and soul chilling laughter ceased. Every eye was turned toward its source. Fifty feet away, a black car had pulled up silently, attesting to its high powered motor and the costliness of the body. Headlights out, it had rolled up unnoticed, to a spot diagonally across the street. The door was open, and a strangely frightful figure stood upon the running board. It was swathed in a black cape from shoulder to heels. A black hat with brim turned far down hid most of the face, except for a pair of gleaming eyes which seemed to burn like beacons of fiery vengeance in the darkness.

Two guns were in the hands of that motionless figure—guns that were held at the hips in a carelessly familiar manner.

Involuntarily, the gunmen shrank back a little against the bus. The thug on the motorcycle sat frozen in his seat. Kinley's jaw dropped when he saw the apparition.

Only Señor Edouardo Estéban spoke. "It is—the Spider!

Gracias à Dios, Señor Spider! I did not think you would come. I had given myself up for dead!"

Kinley uttered a sharp, vicious curse. "The Spider!" He swivelled the submachine gun toward that grim cloaked figure, his finger pressing on the trip. "Take him, guys!"

But the two guns in the hands of the Spider spat first. One shot took Kinley squarely between the eyes. A second hurled the motorcyclist off his machine. The two explosions reechoed like thunder down the lonely street.

And then the Spider laughed once more. His guns swiveled, belching flame and thunder, to meet the quick fusillade from the other thugs. He never moved from his position on the running board of the black car, and his dark figure, merging with the blackness, was a difficult mark for these frightened gunmen to hit.

Frightened? Yes, they were frightened, for they had never before been pitted against those blazing twin automatics of the legendary Spider. But they had heard stories. They had heard that wherever a colossus of crime reared his ugly head to inflict pain and misery upon innocent people, there appeared the Spider. And they had heard, too, that the Spider was a law unto himself, defying even the law of organized society when he waged war upon crime. No criminal had ever faced those blazing automatics and lived to tell the tale.

THEY HAD no stomach for this fight, now that they faced

a grim fighting man instead of a bus full of frightened passengers. But they kept on shooting, like vicious beasts at bay, until the last of them had gone down under the coldly accurate fire of those deadly automatics.

At last the shooting ceased. None of the gunmen remained on his feet.

Once more the Spider laughed. "Have no fear!" he called out to the semi-hysterical passengers. "You will not be harmed." His voice, deep-toned and full-throated, gave them courage and confidence. Their cries died down.

"Thank you," said the Spider. "Always remember that the Spider does not make war upon innocent men and women. You have nothing to fear from me."

One of the automatics disappeared miraculously beneath the black cloak, and he stretched forth a hand toward Edouardo Estéban.

"Come, Señor Estéban. I regret that you received such an ungallant welcome in my country. I shall see to your safety from this moment on. Come with me!"

"Gladly!" cried Señor Edouardo Estéban, as he ran across to the black sedan.

The Spider helped him in, and did not at once follow him. In the distance there sounded a police siren, but it did not seem to cause him to hurry. He crossed to the bodies of the gangsters, lying beside the bus. Swiftly he went from one to the other of them, kneeling for a moment beside each. When he was finished, there was a mark upon the foreheads of all of them—a blood red figure of a Spider.

It was a mark which had often been seen upon the bodies of those criminals who were executed by this grim nemesis of the Underworld. Once more, by that mark, the whole world would know that the Spider was walking again. And in many a dark and slimy corner, the calloused killers, the shock troops of crime, would tremble and curse under their breath.

The cloaked figure crossed back to the black sedan. In spite of the swiftly approaching police siren, he turned and bowed low to the occupants of the bus.

"Goodbye, ladies and gentlemen," he said in his deep and sonorous voice. "I am sorry if you have been caused fear or inconvenience. I trust you will forgive me."

"Forgive you!" exclaimed a woman, leaning out of one of the bus windows. "We should thank you, Spider. We all saw how you fought these murderers. They were going to kill that poor Spanish gentleman in cold blood. You deserve a vote of thanks!"

The Spider bowed once more. "Unfortunately, madam, I dare not remain to receive it. The only thanks I would get from the police would be a quick volley. Goodbye!"

He stepped into the car, and a moment later it glided away, like a ghost in the night.

When the police arrived, moments later, not one passenger

in the bus would vouchsafe information as to which way the Spider had gone.

The black sedan was by this time safely out of Queens County, making its way toward Manhattan in a circuitous manner, by way of Brooklyn. In this way it avoided the necessity of crossing by one of the larger bridges, which would surely be watched.

Señor Edouardo Estéban sat very still, alongside the black caped driver.

"Señor Spider," he said, "once more I owe you my life. It seems that I must always be in your debt. Seven years ago, you saved me from death when I lay helpless at the mercy of *El Crocodilo.* Today, I had hoped to repay that debt, by bringing you information of *El Crocodilo.* But now I am in your debt again."

He spoke in Spanish, and it was in that language that the Spider answered him.

"Never think it, Don Estéban. I owe you safety in this country. And you would not have risked your life at all, had you not come to warn me of *El Crocodilo.* So let us say that we are quits. But tell me quickly—what is this information about *El Crocodilo?*"

DON ESTEBAN sighed. "Once before, *El Crocodilo* came north to make a try for power. It was you, Señor Spider who defeated his ambition. For seven years now, *El Crocodilo* has nursed thoughts of revenge—and of power. Today, I fear, he is strong enough to succeed!"

"Do you mean," demanded the Spider, "that he is in New York again?"

"Indeed, yes. Those were his men, at the bus. He has agents

everywhere, thousands of them, all lured by high pay, and the promise of great wealth."

The Spider drove skillfully, without effort. He was free to concentrate upon what Don Estéban told him.

"What does *El Crocodilo* plan this time?"

"He intends to become the master of all the financial institutions in America!"

"Impossible, Don Estéban. It has been tried by greater men than he. There is too much money in America. No one man can control it."

Don Estéban laughed hollowly. For answer he took a sheaf of bills from his pocket and handed one to the Spider.

"Examine it!"

The Spider turned on a dashboard light, and held the bill under it. He slowed down to a crawl while he examined the bill, turning it around in his gloved fingers. At last he said, "It's genuine, Don Estéban. It's a hundred dollar bill, and it's good American money."

Once more, the Mexican laughed. "Every bank teller in America would confirm it as genuine, Señor Spider. Even Treasury officials have passed it. But it is counterfeit!"

"Ah!" said the Spider. He drove on now, staring straight ahead. "Go on, Don Estéban," he said softly.

"This is what I have come to tell you, Señor Spider. Seven years ago, when I was destitute and ruined in health by my terrible experience with *El Crocodilo*, you lent me much money, and reestablished my life in Mexico. Your sole condition was that I should keep eternal watch for the reappearance of *El Crocodilo*.

Today I come to pay my debt. I come to tell you that *El Crocodilo* prepares to wage war against your country!"

"How?"

"This, I do not know. My spies have found out about the false money. Also, they have brought me a list of names—here it is. They are the names of American bankers. What it means, I do not know. Perhaps you can understand its significance."

The Spider took the list and held it under the light. Those glittering eyes under the turned down hat brim took on an extra sheen. The list was a carbon copy, evidently one of many neatly typed, and numbered from one to fifteen. The first four were as follows:

1. Everett Masters, 14th Nat'l Bank
2. John Power, Bank of Greeley Square
3. Franklin Boyce, Retailers' Trust
4. Norton Vandercook, International Export Bank

The list went on to enumerate fifteen of the leading banks in the city, with their presidents.

The Spider's black gloved hand crushed the sheet of paper, and stuffed it into a pocket.

DICTATOR'S DEATH-MERCHANTS

"You know what this list means, Don Estéban?" he asked harshly.

"But yes, Señor Spider. It is just now that I have heard the radio talk. Three banks have already been destroyed. I pray that you may save the rest. You must speak with the presidents of those banks which have been demolished—"

"That is impossible, Don Estéban," the Spider broke in. "The presidents of those banks are dead. Everett Masters and John Power were murdered. Franklin Boyce committed suicide!"

"Madre de dios!" exclaimed the Mexican. "This *El Crocodilo*—he is too clever—and ruthless!"

"We shall see!" the cloaked driver said grimly. "But first, you must go into hiding, lest the long arm of *El Crocodilo* reach for you once more. Come. I will see to it that you are well hidden!"

THE CAR was now in Manhattan, and the Spider drove swiftly uptown, keeping to the darker streets. The shortwave radio on the dashboard was sputtering as a police announcer's voice crackled: *"Attention, all cars! Alarm for the Spider! He has just killed six men and abducted another. Believed cruising somewhere in Queens, but may be heading toward Brooklyn, or one of the Manhattan Bridges. Shoot on sight...."*

Don Estéban groaned. "I see it is as always, Señor Spider. Whatever you do, it is twisted into a bad thing. These police are fools. Come to Mexico, Señor. There, you will be hailed as a hero. As for me, though I have never seen your face, I would trust you with my life!"

The Spider laughed grimly. "My work is in this country, Don

Estéban. I am an American. And thanks or no thanks, I serve the American people in my own way!"

Don Estéban fell silent. The Spider drove for a few minutes longer, and then made a right turn into a factory street, dark and deserted now. He pulled the black sedan to a stop in front of a factory building upon which there was a large. "To Let" sign.

"There is one thing more I would like to know, Don Estéban. It is seven years since I have seen the face of *El Crocodilo.* Would I know him now?"

"No, Señor, you would not know him. His face has been changed by a skillful surgeon. But *I* have seen his new face. It is a reason why they have wished to kill me. I, alone, can identify him."

"All the more reason," the Spider said grimly, "to keep you safe!"

He swung the car into a driveway alongside the factory building. At the end of the driveway, there was the reinforced steel door of a large garage attached to the factory. This door opened automatically when the Spider reached out of the window and pressed a certain spot in the adjoining wall. The car rolled inside, into total darkness. The steel door descended slowly into place, on greased and noiseless skids.

The Spider and the man he had saved were lost to the sight of the world.

Fifteen minutes later, a snappy blue convertible coupé rolled out of a garage in the back street, immediately behind the factory building. The driver of that coupé in no way resembled the cloaked, sinister figure of the Spider. On the contrary he was a well dressed, immaculately groomed gentleman, handsome and debonair, and apparently without a care.

Nevertheless, his eyes were keen and penetrating as he glanced up and down the street to make sure he was not observed. After making sure on this point, he swung the costly coupé to the right, and turned the corner, heading uptown.

Ten minutes later, he parked in front of a magnificent apartment building on Park Avenue. The doorman nodded with genuine deference as he held the door open for him.

"Good evening, sir. It's a pleasure to see you, sir."

"Thank you, Tom. Please phone upstairs to the penthouse and tell Mr. Vandercook that Mr. Richard Wentworth is here on a matter of vital importance!"

CHAPTER 2
EL CROCODILO'S FIRST MOVE

IN LESS than three minutes Richard Wentworth was being ushered into the Louis XIV sitting room of Norton Vandercook, President of the International Export Bank, and number four on the list of a certain *El Crocodilo.*

Norton Vandercook was an impressive man, both in bearing, in manner and achievement. Though he was the chief executive of a hundred million dollar bank, he had simple tastes, as did his frail and kindly wife. Her pure gray hair and the delicate texture of her skin made a pleasing contrast to Vandercook's ruddy, vigorous appearance. They both greeted Richard Wentworth cordially, and he bent with all the courtly grace of an old-world courtier, to kiss Mrs. Vandercook's hand.

She sighed, and patted him on the arm. "I'll leave you with Norton now. I can see you're aching to talk to him privately." She shook her head sadly. "You men! Must it always be business with you?"

As soon as she was gone from the room, Norton Vandercook's easy manner of geniality dropped from him like an actor's mask.

"Dick!" he exclaimed. "I'm glad you came tonight. There are three vultures—human vultures—after me. I need your help!"

"Call on me for anything, Mr. Vandercook!"

The older man paced up and down nervously. "You know what happened to Masters, and Power, and Boyce, of course. I'm afraid the same thing will happen to International Export as happened to those other three banks. And that I'll meet the fate of their presidents."

"You've been threatened?"

"Not directly. But there's a syndicate consisting of three men who demand that I sell them my stock in the International Export Bank. They're coming here tonight for an answer. They're a queer crew, Dick—a German, a Russian and a Jap. Hans Schmidt is a German industrialist who backed the Nazi party with his millions, and who has been recently kicked out of Germany. The Russian is a former Russian munitions broker named Boris Roganov. The Jap is Baron Toyo Niti, who financed a large portion of the Japanese invasion of China, and is now out of favor in Japan."

Wentworth nodded thoughtfully. “I’ve heard of all three, of course. So they’re working in this country now!”

“There’s somebody behind them, Dick—somebody so powerful and ruthless that I—I’m frightened. Look what they did to the others who refused to sell!”

“It would be interesting to meet these three gentlemen!” Richard Wentworth said softly.

“They’re due here any minute—”

Vandercook was interrupted by the butler, knocking at the door. “The three gentlemen you are expecting, sir—Herr Schmidt, Mr. Roganov, and Mr. Niti.”

“Show them in!” said Vandercook.

When the three men entered, their eyes swiveled as one to Richard Wentworth.

Herr Hans Schmidt was a powerful man with small eyes, close-cropped hair, and a Prussian moustache. Roganov was much the oldest of the three. He carried his head tilted on one side, so that he looked like an ancient and obscene bird of prey, waiting to pounce down and gnaw at a victim’s vitals. Baron Toyo Niti was small boned, almost dainty, yet with the look of a swamp adder in his small, almond eyes.

It was Roganov who spoke for all of them. He placed a black leather valise on the table, and motioned toward it.

“We ’ave brought the cash, Mr. Vandercook. Seven ’undred thousand dollars—for your controlling stock in the International Export Bank.”

“Seven hundred thousand!” exclaimed Vandercook. “My stock is only worth half a million—”

Roganov smiled a mealy smile, and spread his hands in a wide gesture. "We give you a good profit, Mr. Vandercook. And all in cash!"

He opened the valise, and displayed the bundles of currency.

"Just a minute," Wentworth said politely. He stepped forward and picked up one of the bundles. It consisted of hundred dollar bills. They looked genuine—as genuine as the ones which Edouardo Estéban had showed him only a little while ago. Yet he had Estéban's assurance that these bills were counterfeit.

HE LOOKED up and saw that Vandercook was watching him. He shook his head slightly in the negative.

Vandercook smiled. He faced the three vultures.

"Gentlemen," he said, "I have decided not to sell!"

"W'at!" exclaimed Roganov. "You refuse such a profit?"

"Yes!"

The three vultures exchanged little secret glances. Hans Schmidt leaned over and whispered something to Roganov. The Russian shrugged and began to close the valise.

"Excuse me!" said Wentworth. He put his hand on the lid of the valise, preventing the Russian from closing it. "I am wondering," he said very slowly, "whether this money is genuine. Perhaps we should have it checked by Treasury officials."

Roganov stepped back a little from the table. Schmidt and Niti became suddenly tense and watchful. They spread out a bit to the right and left of the table, and Niti's hand stole into his pocket.

Wentworth smiled apologetically. "I've been stuck with a couple of counterfeit hundreds in the last few days myself, and these bills in your valise look like them." He reached for the telephone. "I'll just call a friend of mine in the Treasury Department, and ask him to run over—"

Toyo Niti's hand came out of his pocket like a flash. It was gripping a small automatic. At the same time, Hans Schmidt lunged at Wentworth, raising a blackjack which was attached to his wrist by a leather thong.

Dick Wentworth snatched the valise, and flung it full into Schmidt's face. The big man collided with it, head on, and packets of money went flying all over the room, the bands breaking and scattering the bills like oversized confetti.

Toyo Niti's purpose had been only to cover Dick so that Schmidt could strike him down without opposition. But now he drew in his breath with a sharp, hissing sound, and thrust the automatic forward, as the hundred dollar bills showered through the air, and Schmidt went staggering backward under the impact of the valise.

Wentworth leaped to one side, in the other direction, and seized Boris Roganov by the collar. The fat Russian had moved too slowly to produce a weapon, though he was fumbling in his pocket for one. He squealed and squirmed as Wentworth whirled him around.

The Jap hesitated just a second when he saw Roganov's bulk interposed between himself and his target. And in that moment, Wentworth gave the Russian a powerful shove that sent him stumbling straight at Niti. Niti swung his hands up to ward off the stout man's body, and that was all Dick Wentworth needed. Before any of the three had recovered from his swift counterattack, he had a heavy black automatic out of his shoulder holster. He took a single step forward and brought the barrel down sharply upon Toyo Niti's wrist. The Jap bleated, let his gun drop to the floor.

Wentworth smiled, and stepped back. He swung the automatic to cover all three.

"And now, gentlemen," he said, "we will proceed to call my friend in the Treasury Department!"

He glanced at Norton Vandercook, who had stood transfixed through the swift and silent scuffle.

"Mr. Vandercook," Wentworth asked, "will you kindly pick up the phone and call Rector Two, Nine-one-O-O? That's the Secret Service Division of the Treasury Department. Ask for Mr. Grimsby, the night superintendent!"

AS IN a daze, Norton Vandercook approached the table and reached for the instrument. Being a banking executive, he was unused to scenes of violence. He was still trying to comprehend what had happened in those few short moments of kaleidoscopic action.

Hans Schmidt was standing in a sort of semi crouch, his small eyes lancing hatred at Wentworth There was blood upon his forehead, where the edge of the valise had opened the skin. But he did not bother to wipe it off. He was awaiting an opportunity to jump Wentworth once more. The blackjack still dangled from his wrist. Roganov was picking himself up from the floor, where he had fallen, while Niti was nursing an injured wrist. None of them had spoken.

But now, just as Vandercook had his hand on the phone, Roganov said hastily, "Wait, Mr. Vandercook! Do not'ing rash!"

"Rash?" Vandercook looked at him with a frown. "What do you mean? You men came here to trick me into selling you my stock in exchange for counterfeit money. I am certainly going to take Mr. Wentworth's advice—"

"Per'aps you weel wait," Roganov glanced at the watch on his fat wrist, "for only two or t'ree minutes. He straightened his clothing, and smiled with the greatest of assurance. "You mus' know that Herr Schmidt an' Mr. Niti an' myself are not fools. We 'ave not come 'ere wit'out protection for such a t'ing as this." He waved toward Wentworth's steady gun.

"What do you mean?" Vandercook asked.

Roganov explained, smilingly. "It is now two minutes of eight. At eight sharp we are to telephone to a certain party. If 'e do not 'ear from us, 'e will phone 'ere. I wish that you talk wit' 'im—before you call the Treasury Department."

Vandercook looked with uncertainty at Wentworth Dick frowned. "Who is this certain party who is going to phone?" Dick asked.

Roganov's eyes flickered. "You shall see."

"Would it be—*El Crocodilo?*"

The Russian stiffened. He exchanged swift glances with Niti and Schmidt. "Per'aps," he said.

"All right," Dick decided. "We'll wait."

The seconds seemed to tick away so slowly that each minute was like an hour. The clock on Vandercook's desk at last showed eight sharp. The second hand began to move around its circle, but before twenty seconds more elapsed, the phone rang!

Its sharp clang electrified everyone in the room.

Norton Vandercook snatched it up. "Yes?" he said. "This is Mr. Vandercook speaking."

A voice came over the phone so metallic and sharp that it was audible to everyone in the room.

"Vandercook? Why haven't I received a call from Roganov?"

Vandercook frowned. "Who is this?"

"You may call me—*El Crocodilo*—the Crocodile. I ask you one question—have you sold your stock?"

"No, damn you. And we're going to put these three men of yours behind bars—"

"Not so fast, my dear Vandercook. I have planned too well for that. You will not have Roganov and Schmidt and Niti arrested. No."

"That's where you are mistaken!" the banker barked. "I shall certainly do so! And we'll get you, too!"

"I don't think so. Not when I remind you that you have a very beautiful daughter named Ellen—whom you love very much!"

Vandercook's face went white. "What—what about Ellen?"

"She attends Vauxhall College, doesn't she?"

"Yes."

"Weren't you notified by the college authorities that your daughter hadn't slept in the dormitory last night?"

"Y-yes. But—but I thought she might have gone to visit friends in town—"

THERE WAS a harsh metallic laugh from the other end of the wire. "She isn't visiting friends, my dear Vandercook. She's *my* guest! She's in a place where she'll never be found—unless I return her to you. If, by any chance, the place *should* be discovered, it would be destroyed by a demolition bomb just like the ones that have wrecked the banks of your friends. Your daughter is in that place, in chains, my dear Vandercook. She's guarded by faithful Yucatan Indians who obey me to the letter. I leave the rest to your imagination!"

"You devil!" shouted Vandercook. "If you harm her—"

"She will not be harmed, my friend, unless you prove unreasonable. I ask only that you quietly sell your stock to my friends—"

"For counterfeit money?" Vandercook interrupted bitterly.

"Ah! So you know that. Well, you must even do that. In four days more, I will control the whole financial structure of America, and I will decree that the money my agents are using shall be accepted as genuine. You have nothing to lose. Your daughter will be returned safely at the end of the four days. I shall hold her till then, to make sure you reveal nothing of all this to the police. And now, goodbye!"

The click of the phone indicated that *El Crocodilo* had hung up. Norton Vandercook's face was bathed in sweat as he put down the phone. Roganov, Schmidt and Niti were watching him, with little triumphant smiles on their faces.

Dick Wentworth's pulse was racing. This then, was the proof that everything Don Estéban had told him was true. That had been *El Crocodilo* at the other end of the telephone. And these three vultures were agents of *El Crocodilo.* Yet looking at Norton Vandercook's drawn and agonized face, Wentworth knew that nothing must be done to these three—while Ellen Vandercook was in the power of *El Crocodilo.*

Vandercook said brokenly, "I—I'll have to do what they ask, Dick!"

Wentworth nodded, silently. But he did not lower his automatic.

Vandercook turned to the three vultures. "Gentlemen," he said, "tomorrow afternoon I will deliver to you the stock certificates covering my controlling shares of the International Export Bank!"

Roganov smiled his mealy smile. Schmidt continued to scowl. Toyo Niti murmured, "So sorry for all the trouble!"

The three of them backed out of the room, leaving the money strewn all over the floor.

"We shall return," Roganov said at the door, "tomorrow."

Hardly had they left, when there was the patter of footsteps, and frail little Mrs. Delia Vandercook entered. Her lips were quivering, but she was holding her head high by a sheer effort of will.

"I—heard!" she said, chokingly.

She came into the room, swaying, and Wentworth helped her to a chair.

Where another woman might have collapsed, or gone into hysterics, this delicate little woman's breeding kept her erect. Dry-eyed, she looked at her husband.

"We must do whatever they say, Norton. We must... take no chance of Ellen's being... harmed."

She turned her tightly controlled face up to Wentworth, "And you, Dick—you must promise not to breathe a word of this."

"I promise!" said Wentworth.

He didn't know, when he said those two words, how much they were going to cost him within a short space of time. But, had he known, he would still have said them to that fine old lady.

He bowed once more over her hand. "I must go, now. For whatever help you need, please don't hesitate to call upon me—or Nita."

"Must you go?" Vandercook asked brokenly. "We—we'll be so—lonely with no one to reassure us... while we wait for tomorrow."

"I must go," Wentworth said gently. "There are... things to which I must attend!"

CHAPTER 3
MAN WITH THE NOTE

DURING BUSINESS hours, there is probably no more crowded and bustling part of the world than the lower Broadway section of New York City, from City Hall down to the

Battery. In those few blocks of towering buildings are located a majority of the financial and shipping institutions of the country, employing hundreds of thousands of office workers.

But, as evening approaches, the great canyon of Broadway spews forth its multitude of little human beings, and sends them scurrying in all directions for home. By seven o'clock the street is quiet; by eight, it is silent; by nine, deserted.

Thus it was that there was no one to notice the queer, scrabbling shape which seemed to be clinging to the face of the great International Export Bank Building, between the forty-eighth and forty-ninth floors. Even if any of the infrequent pedestrians had thought to look up in that direction, the gloom of night would have made it appear to be merely a blotch upon the wall, or perhaps a grotesque shadow.

But to anyone near enough to observe closely, it would have become evident that this apparition was descending by means of a rope from the forty-ninth floor window, which was in darkness. The one directly beneath it, however, was lighted. A faint shaft of illumination from that window highlighted the descending figure for an instant, revealing it to be a man. He was letting himself down, hand over hand, cautiously and noiselessly, so as not to alarm the person who sat at the desk in the room below. Furthermore, the same shaft of light glinted ominously upon the bright and gleaming steel dagger which the climber held clamped in his teeth.

The agility and strength of this climber must have been remarkable, for he was able to maintain his hold upon the rope and yet to so manipulate with his feet that he slid down *along-*

side the window, instead of directly in front of it, where he might have been seen.

Inside that office on the forty-eighth floor, a man with gray hat sat at a desk with his back to the window. His face was lined, his eyes dull and hopeless. The fine high forehead was corrugated with worry as his unaccustomed fingers pecked out letters upon a portable typewriter set on the desk. This man was Norton Vandercook.

A discreet knock sounded at the door.

Norton Vandercook stopped typing, and pressed a button at the side of the desk, which automatically released the catch on the door. It was opened, and a young man poked his head in, deferentially. It was Peter Felton, Vandercook's private secretary. Young Felton had a puzzled and worried look on his face.

"The—the police are here, Mr. Vandercook. Commissioner Kirkpatrick, and two detectives. The Commissioner says that you asked him to come at nine o'clock this evening."

Norton Vandercook sighed. "Quite so, Felton. I did make the request. Have any of the bank directors arrived yet?"

"Six of them, sir. They're all talking quite excitedly with Commissioner Kirkpatrick. They've been at me to tell them what you wanted them for, sir, but—but I'm as much in the dark as they are." Felton's eyes were almost like those of a dog whose master has reprimanded it. He was hurt because his employer had not taken him into his confidence.

Vandercook's hands were trembling, but he kept his face under control. "I shall have an announcement of great importance to make to them in a few minutes, Felton. You say six of the directors are here?"

"Yes, sir."

"Is Mr. Richard Wentworth among them?"

"No, sir. As you recall, you asked Mr. Wentworth to come at nine sharp. It's still ten minutes till nine, and you know how punctual Mr. Wentworth always is. He'll be here on the stroke of nine, I'm sure—"

"Yes, yes, of course. Please send him in as soon as he arrives. I want a few words with him alone before—before I face the others."

"Y-yes, sir," Felton stammered. Then, diffidently, "If—if there's anything *I* can do, Mr. Vandercook, I—I'd be happy—"

"I know, Felton." The aged banker smiled wryly. "But I'm afraid there isn't… anything… that anyone can do. You may go."

The secretary gulped, "Y-yes, sir," and ducked out, closing the door behind him. The catch snapped shut. Norton Vandercook was left alone.

FOR A moment he stared vacantly into space. Then he turned resolutely to the typewriter. Upon the white sheet in the machine he had already written the following:

To the Police and the Directors:

I, Norton Vandercook, beg forgiveness in the sight of God

> for that which I am about to do. It is necessary that I take my own life. This afternoon, I sold all my stock in this institution. I did it to save my daughter's life. But the stock was not mine to sell. It was pledged to the bank, for a large loan. I am, therefore, a thief. I cannot even turn in the amount of money which I received for the stock, because that is counterfeit money. I dare not protest, lest my daughter, Ellen, be tortured to death.
>
> But I have thought carefully about all this. I now know that I must warn the country of what *El Crocodilo* plans for it, even if it means Ellen's death. I know she would want me to do it this way. In writing this, I am practically consigning her to doom. But I shall not survive her. When I have finished this letter, I shall precede her, by leaping from this window....

As he typed, he was unaware of the silent, agile figure which swung onto the window sill, then climbed into the room behind him. He did not hear the killer steal up close behind him, nor did he see the gleaming blade which rose, then swooped down like a bird of prey to bury itself to the hilt between his shoulder blades, nor did he see the hand which simultaneously reached over and snatched the sheet out of the typewriter....

FORTY-EIGHT FLOORS below, a powerful limousine purred to a stop before the entrance of the International Export Bank Building. At the wheel sat the only bearded chauffeur in the City of New York.

A bearded chauffeur would ordinarily be something for other chauffeurs to jibe at, to molest with coarse humor. But no one attempted any levity with this particular chauffeur. The fighting glitter in his dark and leonine eyes and the rippling muscles of his powerful body effectually discouraged any such sallies. Besides, it was well known that he would rather cut off his head than his beard, for he was a member of a fighting race of Sikh warriors, among whom the well-trimmed beard was a mark of caste. In his veins there flowed the blood of kings, of men who had ruled the teeming millions of India before even the white man had learned to write. The name of Ram Singh passed down from father to son for generation upon generation—was still a name to be uttered with bated breath in the wild fastnesses of the Punjab.

That Ram Singh, with all his traditions of pride and caste, should have accepted menial service such as this, was a matter of wonder. But the explanation was simple. The one whom Ram Singh served was the only individual in the entire world whom he acknowledged as the better man. This Sikh warrior, descended from a noble race, was fiercely proud of the privilege of serving Richard Wentworth, and of sharing the one secret whose disclosure would surely cost Wentworth his life.

But neither of them was thinking of that secret at this moment. Ram Singh, as he tooled the limousine in to the curb, glanced anxiously at his watch to make sure that they were not late for the appointment with Norton Vandercook. He nodded in satisfaction, and spoke over his shoulder.

"It is eight minutes before nine, Master. We are early."

"Nice driving, Ram Singh," Wentworth said, from the interior. Then Wentworth turned to Nita van Sloan, who sat beside him. "I don't think I'll be long, darling. But if you'd rather come up—"

"I'd rather wait with Ram Singh," she said. There was an uneasy look in her tawny eyes. Her long, aristocratic hand went out and touched his. "Dick! I have a queer feeling. Something—something terrible is going to happen. I—I wish we hadn't come!"

Wentworth smiled, but he did not laugh.

"I hope you're mistaken this time, darling. It's probably only a routine directors' meeting—"

"Then why did Norton Vandercook call it at such short notice and for nine o'clock in the evening? No, Dick, I'm afraid—afraid that it will be something for—for the Spider!"

Wentworth's lips were grimly tight. "That may be, darling. If it is—it's all the more reason for me to go."

She nodded in resignation. This was the secret which Ram Singh knew, and which she and only two others in America shared with him—that Richard Wentworth, millionaire sportsman, dilettante of the arts and letters, big game hunter and amateur criminologist, was also—the Spider. Whenever a new Napoleon of crime reared his head above the muck of average criminals and laid an ugly shadow across the lives of innocent men and women, then Richard Wentworth ceased to exist, and a cloaked and sinister personality appeared upon the scene—a grim instrument of avenging justice whose twin blazing automatics reached fingers of fiery lead for those master criminals whose cleverness rendered them immune to the blundering, lumbering processes of police law.

AND WHILE the Spider walked in the night upon his avenging mission, the beautiful and aristocratic Nita van Sloan slept not, neither did she eat, for she did not know whether the man she loved would return to her, or whether his broken body lay in some filthy ditch—forfeit at last to the vicious shock troops of the Underworld against whom he pitted his skill and courage.

So she watched him with somber eyes as he stepped out of the limousine. She saw from his attitude that he was poised and wary, all his instincts on the watch for danger. She sensed, too, that it was not alone her warning which had put him thus on his guard. There must be something else then, which he knew and had not told her.

Ram Singh, too, felt the tension in his master's taut figure. Both of them watched him breathlessly. Suddenly it was as if a great clammy hand of evil had reached out to touch them.

Wentworth stood very still for a moment alongside the limousine. His eyes were suddenly glittering and watchful, enveloping and appraising everything upon the quiet street. There were four other costly town cars in front of the building, which he assumed to be those of the other directors of the International Bank, who had already arrived. Parked ahead of the first of these was a black police car, unoccupied. Wentworth tautened as he saw the number of the license plates—Y 15. That was the number of Police Commissioner Kirkpatrick's car.

Kirkpatrick was Wentworth's personal friend, and also his deadliest enemy. For the Commissioner would have risked his life and his fortune to help Richard Wentworth; but he would also have risked his life and his fortune to catch the Spider and sit him in the electric chair.

The presence of Kirkpatrick's car here at this time was indication in itself that Norton Vandercook's call for an emergency meeting of the Board of Directors was fraught with overtones of menace.

But that was not all which Richard Wentworth's keen glance noted and evaluated. For instance, he saw that three of the chauffeurs of the private cars were dozing comfortably at their wheels, but that the chauffeur of the fourth was pacing nervously up and down along the curb, smoking a cigarette with quick and jerky motions, and glancing constantly across the street as if watching for a signal of some sort.

Following that man's glance, Wentworth saw something which he would not otherwise have noticed. A man was walking slowly down the opposite side of the street, with his hands in his pockets, as if he were out for a stroll, with nowhere to go. A second man was leaning negligently against a lamp post a hundred feet beyond. And in the doorway of a store on the opposite side, there was a shadow which was deeper than the others, and which Wentworth made out to be a third man. This third one was doing something peculiar with his hands, which were up close to his face. And as Wentworth's eyes adjusted themselves to the play of light and shadow over there, he felt his blood race as he realized what that third man was doing.

He was holding a pair of binoculars to his eyes, and watching a spot high up on the face of the International Export Bank Building!

Not a muscle of Dick Wentworth's face moved as he arrived at this realization. For at the same instant he noted that the nervous chauffeur had stopped pacing up and down. The man had a swarthy complexion, and beady black eyes under his uniform cap, and he had suddenly stopped pacing, with his cigarette in midair, and was focusing his gaze on the tall and debonair figure of Richard Wentworth.

Dick gave no sign of having noted anything out of the ordinary. He snapped his fingers and exclaimed, "By Jove, I forgot those papers!"

He stepped quickly back into the limousine, and placed a hand over Nita's, pressing it as a signal for silence. At the same time he reached forward and pressed a catch which snapped open the door of a secret compartment in the back of Ram Singh's seat.

"On guard, Ram Singh!" he whispered.

"On guard!" the Sikh repeated with alacrity. Unostentatiously he thrust his hand under his seat and brought out a long barreled revolver, which he held low, out of sight. His eyes glittered with the promise of action and danger.

IN THE meantime Wentworth, with Nita watching him silently, had produced a pair of night glasses from the secret compartment. He pressed another button, and a panel in the top slid back, revealing an opening about three feet square. He tilted his head far back, and placed the night glasses to his eyes. In a moment he had them focused on the blank wall of the bank building. He spotted the lighted window of Vandercook's office high up on the forty-eighth floor, and the powerful lenses clearly showed him the rope dangling from the window above. And even as he got the window lined up in the lenses, he saw a queer, agile figure appear on the sill. It was the figure of a man, but he could not see the face, for it was covered by a turned up coat collar and a low brimmed hat. He saw the figure stuff a paper into a pocket, then seize the rope and swing out, and begin to clamber up toward the window above, hand-over-hand, as agile as a monkey.

Wentworth read the signs right. He groaned aloud.

"Too late!" he exclaimed. "Too late to save Vandercook!" His lips tightened. "But not too late to strike a blow at *El Crocodilo!*"

Nita van Sloan gasped at mention of that name.

"El Crocodilo! Dick! You didn't tell m—"

"No, darling. I had hoped to keep it from you till it was over. Now, I'm afraid it won't be over till many men have died!"

Swiftly, he reached to open the door again. Nita put a hand on his arm. She was breathing fast, her breast rising and falling with apprehension.

"Dick! Then my premonition was correct? The Spider—"

"The Spider walks again tonight!" he told her bleakly.

When he stepped out of the limousine, the swarthy chauffeur was still watching. But the man had not been able to see what took place inside the limousine, for Wentworth had been kneeling on the floor. From Wentworth's face, the chauffeur had no reason to suspect that there was anything amiss. It was one of Richard Wentworth's supreme accomplishments that he had learned how to master the muscles of his face and the motions of his superbly trained body so as never to betray what he felt or thought.

Swiftly he said to Ram Singh in Punjabi, "Be doubly alert, old friend. There is great danger. Do not wait for me. Watch that town car, with the swarthy chauffeur—the one with the Mexican license plates. Follow it wherever it goes. Meet me at the apartment."

"It shall be done, Master!" the Sikh replied in the same language.

Nita called softly after him, "Good luck, Dick!"

But he did not hear her. He was already striding across to the entrance of the building. He did not seem to hurry, yet his long stride carried him swiftly through the lobby to the elevator.

There was one night elevator in service, and the operator sprang to attention when he saw the immaculate evening clothes, the correct Chesterfield, and the expensive Homburg hat of the new arrival.

"You'll be attending the directors' meeting, sir—"

"Never mind that!" Wentworth snapped, swinging into the cage. "Up! Up, man, and fast! To the forty-ninth floor!"

The operator hesitated for only a fraction of a second. When he saw the look in Wentworth's eyes, he gulped, shut the door, and sent the cage up.

"Who would be on the forty-ninth floor now?" Wentworth demanded tensely.

"Why, I guess it would be Mr. Garcia—of the Garcia Importing Company, sir. He brought an auditor in this evening, to go over some special books—"

"Is Garcia's office directly above Mr. Vandercook's?"

"Y-yes, sir."

Richard Wentworth's eyes were bleak. He said nothing more.

The cage snapped past the forty-eighth, and cushioned to a stop at forty-nine.

WENTWORTH STEPPED out into the corridor and said harshly, "Close your door and go down to the forty-eighth. Commissioner Kirkpatrick will be there. Bring him up. Tell him Richard Wentworth wants him up here!"

"Y-yes, Mr. Wentworth!"

The boy was trembling as he slid the door shut.

Dick Wentworth was alone in the corridor. Opposite, was the door of the Garcia Importing Company, number 4960. On the forty-eighth, the offices of the International Export Bank occupied the entire floor. Here, however, the space was broken up into smaller offices, for tenants in other lines of business. The Garcia Importing Company was by no means a small outfit. The double doors of 4960 appeared to lead to spacious offices. Wentworth turned the knob carefully, and found it locked.

He took off his Homburg hat and wrapped it around his fist. Then he smashed the glazed glass in the upper part of the door. He thrust in his arm and released the catch.

Through the broken glass he had a glimpse of the interior of the Garcia offices. There was a spacious outer room, with fifteen or twenty typewriter desks, all unoccupied now. Beyond these desks was the door of Garcia's private office. That door was wide open, revealing the figure of a thickset man with muscular shoulders, who was leaning out of the window and reaching for something which was apparently being handed to him by the man who was climbing up the rope. Wentworth could see the thick hemp knotted around the steam pipe at the side of the window. It was stretched taut.

At the sound of the smashing glass, the thickset man whirled. He had a heavy revolver in one hand, and in the other he was holding the sheet of white paper which he had just been given.

Wentworth pushed the door open, and stepped into the outer office.

The thickset man pointed the revolver at him through the connecting doorway.

"What do you want here?" he asked in a low voice.

Wentworth smiled charmingly, and kept advancing toward him.

CHAPTER 4
DANGLING IN MIDAIR!

"MR. GARCIA?" he asked suavely. "I merely thought you might want some help in hauling your—er—friend up the rope."

"Damn you!" spat Garcia, and pulled the trigger.

The revolver spat flame, and the crashing shot reechoed from the office walls. But strangely enough, Richard Wentworth was no longer in the spot he had occupied a moment ago. In spite of his casual and smiling manner, he had accurately estimated the dangerous qualities of Mr. Garcia. Almost as he finished speaking he had hurled himself to one side, out of line with the doorway to the inner office. The bullet struck the frame of the door whose glass Wentworth had broken.

Wentworth slid to a stop
beside the knife-man...

... and Allesandro Garcia went plummeting to earth!

Dick seized one of the revolving typewriter chairs in front of a desk. He was unarmed, but this would serve his purpose. He whirled it up above him, holding it with both hands, and swung it in the air. He let go of it, and it sailed straight through the doorway of the inner office. He figured that Garcia would come through that doorway on the run in order to shoot again. He did—and the chair smashed into his midsection. The breath went out of Garcia in a whistling *whoosh,* and he staggered backward toward the open window.

Wentworth was already on the run. He had purposely thrown the chair low, for he wished to avoid killing the man, but he had not anticipated that Garcia would be hurled back toward the window. He hurdled the chair and leaped into the inner office just in time to see the other teetering precariously against the windowsill. He had dropped the revolver, but the white sheet of paper was still clutched in his left hand. The blow in the midsection had so weakened him that he had not the strength to seize at anything to keep himself from falling out the window. His face was gray with terror.

Wentworth uttered a gasp and sped forward. The windows were the low, casement type, and Garcia's knees were buckling backward over the sill as Wentworth stretched forth a hand to grasp him.

Garcia's right hand clutched at Wentworth's sleeve in the convulsive grip of a drowning man. The weight of his body was already beyond the sill, and Wentworth's forward impetus contributed to carrying them both straight through the window.

Wentworth snatched for the framework, but Garcia frantically wrapped his left arm around Wentworth's wrist, dragging it away from the frame. They both hurtled into space.

In that split-second Wentworth knew again the sensation of staring into the eyes of Death. More than once he had laughed in the very face of the Grim Reaper. He had no feeling of terror now, or of wild regret. He felt that his life was long ago forfeit to the eager reaching hands of Death. So often had he escaped, that he felt he was living now on borrowed time. That the end must come some day, suddenly and in the least expected fashion, he had always known. Here it was, then, and he was prepared for it.

Whatever he felt in the subconscious, his steel spring mind had not lost its poise. Though he did not see it, he knew that somewhere below the window, there was a hanging rope, and that upon this rope would be a man. With a quick, twisting movement, he yanked one arm free of Garcia's frantic grip. He groped into space—and his fingers touched the coarse strands of hemp.

HIS HAND slid along as he plummeted downward, and his fingers twined around it. There flashed through his mind the thought that this was a futile gesture, for the increased weight of his falling body would surely be too much for his strength to stop. He expected to feel the rope torn from his hand. Nevertheless, he gripped it with all the power he could muster. The rope burned his tight-closed hand like a column of pure fire. And then he stopped falling.

He was hanging in space by his arm, and close beside him, also clinging to the rope, was the killer who had been climbing up.

But fate had not been so kind to Mr. Alessandro Garcia. He plummeted earthward in a wide arc, hurtling end over end like a broken puppet. A terrible, pulsing scream came tearing from his throat when he was about halfway down, and then there was no other sound until he hit the concrete below. *That* sound was one which it is unnecessary to describe.

But Wentworth had no time to worry about Garcia. He was faced with a new and immediate peril. For this man with the thin, sharp featured face was snarling like a beast of prey, and in his hand there had appeared a second dagger, similar to the one with which he had stabbed Norton Vandercook. He had his legs wrapped around the rope, and was clinging to it also with his left hand. The knife was in his right, and he had it raised to drive straight into Richard Wentworth's throat.

Any other man but Wentworth would have been so demoralized by the terrific experience of a moment ago, that he would have been defenseless against the poised knife. Not so, Wentworth. His right hand was tight around the rope, the only thing that kept him from dropping off into space. But his left was already on its way up to ward off the blow. In the cramped quarters, with both of them virtually tied to each other by the necessity of clinging to the rope, there was little room for tricky work. The knifeman knew his advantage, and he meant to press it to the utmost. Also, he must have realized his danger. For the body of Alessandro Garcia had collected a crowd down below. Also, the very fact that Wentworth was here meant that his murder of Norton Vandercook was already discovered, or would soon he

found out. He must kill this interloper swiftly, and make his escape.

Richard Wentworth read that thought in the man's eyes even as his arm came up under the point of the dagger, so that the man's wrist struck his forearm. Wentworth held his arm up in that position, with the killer pressing the point down toward Wentworth's throat, trying to break through the suddenly-erected defense. The point of the dagger was barely two inches from Wentworth's throat, and only the strength of his arm prevented it from being driven home.

Thus, the two men on the rope hung, chest to chest, eye to eye, muscle straining against muscle.

Wentworth swung his legs up around the other's body in a scissors grip. He strained every muscle in his body to hold that hungry knife back from his throat yet he thought with grim humor that it was perhaps the first time in the history of the world that this particular wrestling hold had been executed at the end of a rope, forty-nine stories above the ground.

With his legs wrapped tightly about the other, Wentworth let go his hold upon the rope.

NOW, THE knife-man was supporting them both! The pressure of that knife hand against Wentworth's upraised arm lessened. Wentworth breathed more freely. He smiled sociably into the other's strained and hate-contorted face.

"Relax, my friend," he said. "You're holding both of us up now.

If you want to kill me, all you have to do is let go of the rope, and we'll both go diving down together!"

As he said this he brought his right hand around and seized his opponent's knife wrist. Slowly, inexorably, Wentworth forced his hand back and up, twisting slightly and forcing him to open his fingers. The knife slid out of his grip, clattered against the wall, and then dropped down toward the ground, far below.

"Good!" grunted Wentworth. "Now, my friend, we can talk. There's no escape for you. Will you climb up with me—peaceably?"

He jerked his head upward, and the other followed his gaze. The head of Police Commissioner Kirkpatrick appeared suddenly in the window above.

"Dick!" he called down excitedly. "Good God, what's this?"

Wentworth kept his legs wrapped around the other's body, but he took the precaution of gripping the rope with one hand now. He smiled up crookedly at the Commissioner.

"Is Norton Vandercook dead?"

"Yes, yes. Stabbed in the back. But—but—"

"Here's his murderer, Kirk." He looked soberly at the knife man. "Come on," he said. "We'll go up."

A sudden frantic energy seemed to seize the other. He shouted something in a strange, guttural tongue. Then he untwined his legs from around the rope, and let go his hold. He tried to dive out into space.

Wentworth kept his scissors hold about the other's torso, while he gripped the rope with one hand. But the man was now just as determined to plunge to destruction as he had been to preserve his life a moment ago. He threshed about furiously, trying to break Dick's scissors hold. The strain upon Wentworth's muscles was terrific. He had to take a long chance. He gripped the rope harder with his left hand. With his right fist bunched in a hard knot he chopped down mercilessly against the man's temple. The blow landed with a sickening thud, and the struggling knifeman went limp. Dick's face was white with anguish as he turned his head upwards.

"Hurry, Kirk!"

Commissioner Kirkpatrick had been joined by other men. They united their strength in drawing the rope up, while Wentworth clung to it with both hands, his legs still gripping the unconscious killer. It was a long, almost interminable five minutes before the police succeeded in pulling the two of them over the sill.

WENTWORTH BENT over the unconscious man, with Kirkpatrick alongside him, inspecting the fellow's long, thin face, with the long black hair, and the savage cast of the features.

"Good God," Kirkpatrick said, "what is he? I've never seen such a specimen—"

"He's an Indio, Kirk."

"Indio? What's that?"

"One of the native tribes of South and Central America. They're all called Indios. This one might be a Jivaro, a Chihu, or anyone of a dozen tribes from Yucatan, or maybe even farther south, in the Amazon basin."

"But who—who would bring him—"

Wentworth had already gotten to his feet. "Come on, Kirk.

We mustn't waste time. We've got to get downstairs. That man, Garcia, had a note in his hand when he fell. I think it was a message from Vandercook. We've got to find it before one of *El Crocodilo's* men picks it up!"

Dazed, only half understanding what Wentworth was telling him, Kirkpatrick allowed himself to be dragged to the elevator. The cage was waiting, having just brought up several of the directors from the meeting room below. They called excitedly to both Wentworth and Kirkpatrick, asking for information, but Dick brushed them aside and pulled the Commissioner into the elevator.

"Down!" he rapped.

As the cage shot downward, Wentworth explained rapidly to Kirkpatrick just how he had come to be hanging on to that rope with the desperate knifeman. He learned from the Commissioner that he and the Directors on the forty-eighth floor had heard nothing, not even the sound of Garcia's gun when he had fired at Wentworth. When the elevator operator had come down with Wentworth's message, Kirkpatrick had suspected that something was wrong, and had forced open the locked door of Vandercook's office, only to find him dead at his desk with a dagger between his shoulder blades. It was at that moment that they heard the scream and had seen Garcia's body hurtling down past them.

"But I don't understand how you got up there, Dick," Kirkpatrick finished hurriedly as the elevator jounced to a stop at the main floor. "How do you know *El Crocodilo* is involved?"

"No time to explain now!" Wentworth shouted as the two

of them raced out of the lobby into the street. "We must get our hands on that paper!"

But when they reached the street, Wentworth stopped short, with narrowed eyes. A presentiment of catastrophe chilled him like a cold north wind, for his car was gone from the curb, and with it, Ram Singh and Nita.

Out in the gutter laid the crushed body of Alessandro Garcia. A small crowd consisting of the chauffeurs of the limousines, and one or two passersby were keeping at a respectable distance from the gory remains. However, there was no white paper clutched in the fingers of Alessandro Garcia.

CHAPTER 5
DICK WENTWORTH—FUGITIVE!

AUTOMATICALLY, WENTWORTH also noted that the town car with the Mexican license plates was gone. Likewise, the loiterers across the street were nowhere in evidence. Saying nothing, he kept close to Kirkpatrick's elbow as the Commissioner issued swift orders to a patrolman who had come running over, then turned to question the bystanders.

The chauffeurs all tried to talk at once, excitedly pouring out all their impressions. Listening silently while Kirkpatrick tore his hair, Wentworth learned that almost at the very instant when Garcia's body struck the pavement, a man had darted out from a doorway and snatched something from the dead man's hand. One chauffeur said the object was a scarf, another that it was a book, while a third maintained stoutly that it had been a flowered tablecloth. Wentworth, aware of the notorious inaccuracy of witnesses regarding details, knew that it was the white sheet of typewritten paper which the man had snatched.

That was about all they could learn, except for one thing—a fact which Wentworth elicited by a question of his own. This was that his limousine, with Nita and Ram Singh, had pulled away right after the town car.

Wentworth understood that Nita's quick wit had sent her after that town car, rather than attempt to recover the paper at once. Knowing that it was *El Crocodilo* with whom they had to contend, she must have reasoned that knowledge of the location of his headquarters might be even more important than the immediate recovery of the paper.

But he was worried, for he knew the resourcefulness and the power of *El Crocodilo*. It had been his intention to keep Nita clear of this imbroglio, and he blamed himself for having brought her down here. But the fat was in the fire. In one way or another, she would eventually have managed to inject herself into the midst of danger. At least she had Ram Singh with her, and the Sikh would die rather than allow harm to befall her.

While Kirkpatrick continued to question the witnesses, Wentworth knelt at the side of the dead Garcia. The body was far from pretty. The head was smashed so that it was unrecognizable, and there did not seem to be a single unbroken bone in the rest of the man's body. Gingerly, Dick went through his pockets until he found what he sought. It was a small silver medallion, no larger than a quarter. Upon its surface there was

executed in bas-relief a gruesome reproduction of a South American man-eating crocodile. The jaws of this hideous monster were clamped about the naked body of a slender girl. So realistic was the carving that it seemed almost as if the crocodile's jaws were about to snap the body in half. Beneath the reproduction there was only a number—111.

Grimly, he showed it to Kirkpatrick. "There's your proof, Kirk, that *El Crocodilo* is involved in this. I dare say, when that knifeman upstairs is searched, they'll find a similar medallion on him!"

The Commissioner took the medallion in his hand, and uttered a low whistle. "Garcia was agent number one-eleven. Then *El Crocodilo* must have at least a hundred and ten other agents!"

"More than that!" Wentworth assured him bleakly. "Garcia must have been an important agent—but nowhere near the top!"

Kirkpatrick was looking queerly at Wentworth. "You haven't told me yet how you knew it was *El Crocodilo*. You know more than you're telling me, Dick."

"It was a hunch," Wentworth said evasively.

KIRKPATRICK SMILED cynically, and shook his head. He took Dick by the arm and led him to, one side, away from the detectives who had come to take charge of the body.

"Look here, Dick," he said in a very low voice. "Seven years ago, *El Crocodilo* came to New York and attempted to establish an empire of crime. He almost succeeded, but for the efforts of a certain person—the Spider. The Spider broke up the vicious scheme, and *El Crocodilo* barely escaped with his life. He's been in hiding in Mexico ever since. But he promised that when he was ready, he'd be back to try again—and that he wouldn't fail the next time."

"I remember reading about that," Wentworth said uncomfortably. "I was out of town at the time—"

"Yes, of course!" Kirkpatrick broke in sardonically. "You've been out of town a good deal during the past seven years, haven't you, Dick? In fact, I've noticed that almost every time the Spider appears on the scene, *you're out of town!*"

"What do you mean, Kirk?"

"I mean just this. You and I are friends, Dick. I couldn't ask for a better friend than you've been to me. But I'm a sworn officer of the law. And the Spider is an outlaw. If I catch the Spider, by God, I'll see that he burns in the electric chair—*no matter who he turns out to be!*"

Wentworth avoided the other's eyes. He pretended to utter a bored sigh. "We've been all over that, Kirk, a thousand times. I know how you feel about the Spider. Why bring it up now?"

The Police Commissioner's grip tightened on Wentworth's arm. "You were Johnny-on-the-spot to catch Vandercook's killer just now. You knew that the paper in Garcia's hand was important—so important that *El Crocodilo* had men stationed here to get it should it be dropped by the man on the rope!"

"Well?" Dick asked. "What of it? You ought to thank me for being on the spot."

Kirkpatrick brought his face close to Dick's. "I wouldn't be surprised if the Spider has been watching, all these years, for the return of *El Crocodilo.* I wouldn't be surprised if the Spider had some kind of information system down in Mexico, to keep him informed of any suspicious incidents that would hint of the Crocodile's imminent return. Under those circumstances, who would be most likely to appear on the scene when *El Crocodilo* strikes the first blow of his campaign?"

"The Spider!" Wentworth answered promptly, with a faint, ironical smile tugging at his lips.

"Exactly! But it was *you* who appeared, Dick!"

"So you accuse me of being the Spider?"

"*Are* you?"

For a long minute the two friends stood facing each other, eye to eye. In Commissioner Kirkpatrick's gaze there was mute suspense and agony. More times than one had he asked this same question of Richard Wentworth. It was his duty. Stanley Kirkpatrick was a man to whom duty came first, above every other consideration. He was even stricter with himself than with others, and there was no doubt that even if he had discovered his own son to be the Spider, he would have placed him under arrest and provided the evidence to send him to the electric chair. It was that quality of high responsibility and utter adherence to duty which had made him the greatest Police Commissioner in the history of the city of New York.

WENTWORTH CONTINUED to smile. "Kirk, if I

Water splashed up on all sides like a furious geyser!

weren't your friend, I'd think that you were persecuting me. Why, even the lowest criminal has the right to consult a lawyer before answering questions. Yet you want me to incriminate myself without benefit of legal advice!"

"You don't need legal advice," Kirkpatrick grumbled. "You've got a Bachelor of Laws Degree, and you're a member of the bar, even if you haven't practiced. You could talk rings around any criminal lawyer I know. But you still haven't answered—"

He was interrupted by a red-faced plainclothesman from one of the myriad squad cars that had arrived within the space of a few minutes.

"Commissioner!" the detective gasped. "Quick! The radio! They're calling for you!"

Wentworth and Kirkpatrick hurried over to the squad car, and bent in to listen. The radio was sputtering as the headquarters announcer fairly stumbled over the words in his excitement.

"Calling Commissioner Kirkpatrick! Calling Commissioner Kirkpatrick!"

The Commissioner picked up the microphone of the two-way radio, and barked, "Kirkpatrick standing by!"

"Commissioner!" the announcer's voice crackled. "You're needed down here. The mayor is here in person. He's been looking for you all over—"

"What's the trouble, man?" Kirkpatrick rapped. "Speak up!"

"It's another bank, sir—the First Avenue State Bank. It was wrecked by a demolition bomb at exactly nine o'clock. The worst part of it is that there's a movie theatre next door, and that was wrecked too—three hundred people were injured and scores killed!"

Commissioner Kirkpatrick's face became a terrible, patchy white. He closed his eyes.

"Three hundred people!" he groaned.

"The mayor is leaving for the scene of the accident at once, sir, and he wants you to meet him there."

"All right," Kirkpatrick said brokenly. "I'll leave at once." He flicked off the two-way switch and looked with haggard eyes at Wentworth. "Dick," he said hoarsely, "I'm to blame for the deaths of those people. I'm the Police Commissioner. I should have prevented it. Their blood is on my hands!"

"How could you have prevented it, Kirk?"

"By finding the devil that's doing it! Instead, I had to wait till *you* put a name to him." He stretched out his hand appealingly. "Dick, in God's name, if you know anything more about *El Crocodilo,* tell me. I take back what I just said. Tell me where to lay my hands on *El Crocodilo,* and then I'll resign—so I won't have to worry about you being the Spider!"

Wentworth's heart went out to his friend, but he held himself in check.

"I'm sorry, Kirk. There's nothing I can tell you—now."

"Why in the world is he destroying these banks? What can he gain by such wanton destruction? And where in the world did Vandercook fit into it?"

WENTWORTH SAID nothing. He felt suddenly helpless, isolated. Something was pounding like a sledgehammer at the base of his brain. There must be an answer—a simple answer to those questions. Don Estéban didn't know. Garcia must have known, but he was dead. Vandercook must have known but he, too, was dead and the note he had written was gone. If only Ram Singh and Nita could have some luck there!

"Good God, Dick, can't you think of something?" Kirkpatrick demanded. "Don't you *know* anything? You must have had *some* knowledge, to bring you down here after that paper."

He paused, and drew a deep breath. Then he said solemnly, "Dick, I've got a question you *must* answer. After what's happened tonight, I insist on an answer. *How did you know that El Crocodilo was back in the United States?"*

Wentworth met Kirkpatrick's hot eyes. "From a friend, Kirk. I learned it from a friend."

"Who is this friend?"

"I'm sorry, Kirk. I can't tell you."

"By God, you'll tell me, here and now! Or I'll clap you in jail for withholding vital information!"

Wentworth's heart skipped a beat. He saw that Kirkpatrick meant his threat, and there was no way out. He couldn't talk, and he couldn't explain. Escape? The street was full of police, now. There were squad cars along the curb, and a morgue wagon had pulled up in the middle of the street. They were just finishing loading the body of Alessandro into it. Also, there were reporters, cameramen, and a crowd of curious bystanders. Egan, the detective who had called Kirkpatrick was standing just a few feet away.

Dick knew just how stubborn his friend, Kirkpatrick could be. And he couldn't blame him much, under the circumstances. Faced with that bit of terrible news which had just come over the radio, it was easy to understand that the Commissioner would be frantic to get whatever information he could. It would be useless to appeal to his sense of fairness, to say that he was bound by his word to keep the secret of a man who trusted him. For the man whose secret he kept—was wanted by the police!

"I have nothing to say, Kirk!" he repeated quietly.

The other's eyes flashed angrily. "Very well, Dick. By your own admission you've placed yourself in the position of concealing evidence. I must do my duty!" He raised his voice. "Egan! I want you to take Mr. Wentworth into custody! Book him on a charge of—"

That was as far as he got. Dick Wentworth sprang back from the running board of the squad car, and sprinted past the astonished Egan before the detective realized what was happening.

BEHIND HIM, Kirkpatrick's voice rose in a hoarse shout of anger.

"Stop, Dick! Stop, I tell you!"

Wentworth paid no attention. He left the sidewalk and ran diagonally out into the middle of the street, behind the squad car. His plan was made in the twinkling of an eye, and he was grimly determined to gamble everything for his liberty. To go to jail now would be disastrous.

The Commissioner's voice rose high in fury.

"Stop him! Stop him!"

Escape seemed impossible. Two bluecoats were directly ahead of him, in the middle of the street, and at Kirkpatrick's shout they turned and crouched, waiting for Dick to come abreast of them. One of them had no weapon in his hands, but the other had a night stick raised, to bring down upon his head when he came within reach.

Wentworth kept coming at them. When he was three feet away, the nightstick came down in a wide swing toward his head. But Dick launched himself into a low, flying tackle that carried him under the club. He spread his arms wide and seized a leg of each patrolman. Then he brought his arms together, and both uniformed men tumbled on top of him.

Dick's legs straightened as he pistoned himself up to his feet, shucking the two cops off him with a tremendous heave. For an instant he was clear of both of them, and he kept on running.

To those officers in the street, and perhaps to Kirkpatrick, too, it seemed that his attempt to escape was futile. There were men ready to block him whichever way he turned. At the Commissioner's shouted orders they began to close in on Dick from all sides, some bringing out night sticks, while the plainclothesmen reversed their guns. They all knew who he was, and presumed that Kirkpatrick would not want him wounded.

Wentworth reversed himself, and doubled back toward the middle of the street, where the morgue wagon stood, with the body of Garcia inside. The men from the morgue wagon had been drawn away in pursuit of him, and now there was only the driver, standing near the left front fender.

That had been Wentworth's purpose from the beginning, and Kirkpatrick must have guessed it now, for he shouted, "Don't do that, Dick, or—*by God, I'll shoot!*"

Wentworth paid him no attention. He was abreast of the driver now, and the man was frantically fumbling for the gun in his shoulder holster. Dick hit him on the run, and sent him sprawling.

"Sorry, old man!" he shouted, and sprang up into the driver's seat of the hearse.

A shot whistled past his head and pierced the windshield, making a flowery star of cracks in the glass. Grimly, Wentworth realized that Kirkpatrick was as good as his word. He was shooting.

Dick switched on the ignition and shifted from first to second, keeping his head low. Two more shots skimmed past him, and then he was heading south, giving the engine all the gas it would take. A small group of policemen ran forward to head him off, but Wentworth kept his foot all the way down on the gas, and the cops scattered. He heard more shots clatter against the body of the car, and held his breath lest a tire be hit. But the tires escaped, miraculously, and in a moment he had left behind the confused and raucous medley of shouts. The hearse careened wildly, and he could hear the body of Garcia jouncing around inside. He shifted into high and the speeding machine covered two, three, four blocks. The speedometer pushed up to sixty, then to seventy.

That was as fast as the car would go. But he realized with a suddenly sinking heart that it wasn't fast enough. Looking in the rear vision mirror he saw a whole procession of cars in pursuit. In the lead was Kirkpatrick's squad car, with Detective Egan on the running board, with his arm outstretched and his service revolver belching flame.

FOLLOWING THAT lead car were others, and though Wentworth wasn't able to give much attention to the rear vision mirror, he thought he saw an automatic rifle in the hands of one of the officers on the running board of the second car.

There wasn't much chance. He was heading straight down Broadway, and in a few blocks they'd be at the Battery, with the bay to cut off further flight. To make a turn at this speed would be death, and to slow up would give the pursuit a chance to close up and place their shots with greater accuracy. A single slug in a tire would send the hearse crashing end over end, to finish up in a pile of twisted junk. And even if he should succeed in making a turn successfully, they were close on his heels, and there were probably other radio cars converging from all directions. They'd cut him off in no time.

Luckily, there was virtually no traffic on lower Broadway at this time of night and his sole problem was to keep the morgue wagon on an even keel at this unaccustomed speed. It had never been built for such strain, whereas the pursuing cars were made to attain speeds of ninety and a hundred miles an hour.

Egan had stopped shooting now, either because his gun was empty, or because it was plain to be seen that they would catch him easily enough without firing a shot. At the Battery, the chase would be over. They could fan out and bottle him up, and have him cold.

Wentworth held the wheel firmly, and did not lift his foot from the accelerator as he flashed past Bowling Green. At the next corner he almost ran down an excited cop, who had heard the approaching sirens and had pulled his gun. Wentworth had to swerve sharply to the right to avoid hitting the man, and he almost lost control of the car. The thing bucked under his hands, but he refused to slow up. It mounted the curb, smashed a hydrant with a crash, and then he fought it back to the road, with Kirkpatrick's car a good fifty feet nearer.

Now, the Battery was visible down the long ribbon of Broadway. Another dozen blocks, and that was all. He had made his choice, had cast the die. By electing to escape, he had brought all the forces of the law after him. But he had chosen odds which were too great. He was beaten. But that quality of high adventure and firm resolve once more asserted itself in the breast of Richard Wentworth. Call it stubbornness, call it pride, call it what you like. Wentworth decided that he wouldn't be taken alive!

He kept that car hurtling down Broadway, straight into Battery Park, leading the racing procession of screeching sirens.

He swung around the bit of green, and headed straight onward for the embankment!

In the rear vision mirror he could see Egan, on the running board of the first car, waving frantically, and shouting to Kirkpatrick to slow up. At the rate they were going, it was manifestly impossible for Wentworth to stop in time to prevent the car from going over into the sea. But the pursuing machines still had a half minute's time in which to save themselves, either by applying the brakes, or turning sharply.

Kirkpatrick stepped on his brakes, and the cars behind, taken by surprise, crashed into his rear end. There was a succession of smashing sounds, as one after the other of the police cars telescoped into the ones in front. For a moment, all attention was taken from Wentworth.

He had reached the embankment, still going at sixty. The front wheels hit the low buttress, and jumped over it, jerking the hearse up into the air. Then the rear wheels skimmed the parapet, and the machine struck the sea.

Water splashed up on all sides like a mighty, furious geyser. The sound of the machine hitting the surface of the sea was like a sharp clap of thunder.

Wentworth, taut and tense, had taken one hand from the wheel, and wrenched open the door. Just as the hearse struck, he let go the wheel entirely, and catapulted himself out of the driver's compartment.

NO ONE saw him jump, for they were occupied with their own crackups. Wentworth was engulfed by the suddenly angry and turbulent waters, which were being churned up like molten lava. The hearse slid down under the water with a sinister, sucking sound, and the undertow dragged Wentworth straight down, as if he were in the center of a whirlpool.

He had expected that to happen, and had filled his lungs with air. Now, as he felt himself carried down, down, he relaxed utterly, allowing his arms to dangle above his head, and his legs to go limp. He was being dragged down in the wake of that hearse, and he did not know how deep the bay was here. However, he knew there was a network of telephone and electric cables here, running from Manhattan out to Staten Island. If only he could break his forced descent on those....

The pressure was becoming terrific. Slowly, he exhaled the breath from his lungs, and held his diaphragm firmly compressed, to keep from inhaling. If he had missed the cables, he was doomed. The best he could hope for would be for his unconscious body to return to the surface, where he might be revived by artificial respiration—only to be arrested.

Suddenly, his foot touched something firm!

It was the bulk of the hearse, which had come to rest on the cable network!

Still holding his diaphragm compressed, he kicked out with

both feet, and sent himself upward. As he rose, he felt the pressure of the water gradually diminishing. And then he broke surface!

He drew in a short, sparing breath of air, not daring to fill his lungs completely, lest he get the bends. Then he kicked over on his back and floated, while strength flowed back into his muscles.

He became aware of a bedlam of noise on the shore, and saw the crowd of police lining the embankment. They were all shouting and gesticulating, and some of them were reaching for flashlights, while others were running back to roll a car up to the edge so they could turn the headlights on the spot where he had sunk.

They hadn't seen him yet, but in a moment someone was bound to detect the white blur of his face in the darkness.

He rolled over, and dived, just as a pair of bright headlights flicked on, and sent gleaming shafts of brilliance across the dark waters.

He swam under water until he got out of the field of light, and then broke surface once more. He gulped air, got his direction, and went under once more. This time he swam toward shore. Ten strokes and he came up. He heard Kirkpatrick's voice, above all the others.

"My God, he'll drown down there. He's locked in the hearse. Get a barge with a crane. We've got to lift it out!"

Grimly, silently, Wentworth swam at an angle, which carried him to the embankment at a spot behind the aquarium building. He climbed onto a pier, and lay flat on his stomach in the darkness. It was a shame to let Kirkpatrick worry like that, until the hearse was raised. But he couldn't very well shout out to them that he was safe. He crawled along the pier in his wet and dripping clothes, until he reached the rear of the aquarium. Then, in the shadow of the building, he stood up.

He heard the clanging sound of fire engines. Someone had summoned them, no doubt with the hope that they could erect an emergency rig to raise the morgue wagon. The Battery was filled with police and with crowds which had gathered, as if by a miracle, from nowhere. It would be impossible for him to make his escape from here, undetected. The minute he stepped out from the shadow of the aquarium building, his dripping clothes would be spotted. It was imperative that he obtain other clothes.

He inched along the wall carefully, until he found a window. He raised it cautiously, and climbed over into the building. There was a small night light burning, and he saw that he was in the rear corridor. To his left there was a staircase down into the basement. His eyes gleamed, and he hurried down, leaving a trail of glistening drops on the stairs!

IN THE locker room he found what he sought—an aquarium guard's uniform. There were five of them to choose from, for the guards were in the habit of changing to civilian clothes before going home. He selected the largest one, and found that it fit him quite well. He stripped to the skin, dried himself with a towel from one of the lockers, and then put the uniform on without underwear. He hung his wet evening clothes up very neatly in the locker, and penciled a short note:

"Keep these as a gift from Richard Wentworth. The money is to pay for a new uniform."

He folded the note, with five ten dollar bills in it, and placed it in the breast pocket of the tuxedo, where it would readily be found. After transferring all his possessions to his new uniform, he went carefully up the stairs, keeping an eye out for the night watchman. He climbed out the window again, shut it punctiliously, and then walked boldly around to the front of the building, drawing the uniform cap low over his forehead.

He found himself in the midst of a maelstrom of activity and feverish noise. Men were hurrying everywhere, shouting orders, advice and information. Fire engines were pulled up close to the embankment, and there was a pulmotor truck and an ambulance from Gouverneur Hospital, with white coated interns waiting to administer first aid.

They were hooking chains on to the rear end of a big fire truck, with the intention of grappling the sunken hearse and dragging it up by the sheer power of the fire engine motor. Police reserves had come up, and they were forming a cordon around the water front, to keep the crowd from pressing too close.

Wentworth walked nonchalantly up to the cordon, and a cop looked at his aquarium uniform and grinned. "Are we disturbing your fish?" he jibed.

"Naw," Wentworth said, "you can go right ahead. The fish like the excitement. I'm gonna get a cup of coffee." He passed through the cordon. At the north end of Battery Park were a couple of idle cab drivers. Wentworth got into one of the taxis.

He gave an address only a few blocks from his home. It was imperative now that he get in touch with his apartment. He must talk to Jackson, his manservant and comrade-at-arms. He must arrange to establish a system of communications, for from now on he would be a hunted man, and he must carry on his campaign against *El Crocodilo* from cover.

At a single stroke, he had made it impossible for himself to appear any longer as Richard Wentworth. And there would be double danger, for the news of this quarrel with Kirkpatrick was now a public matter, and the cause of it would be known. *El Crocodilo* would learn that Wentworth had certain information, and would put two and two together. He would reason such information could only have been gleaned from Don Estéban having talked to the Spider—Richard Wentworth must be the Spider!

For himself, Wentworth was willing to acknowledge the danger of the situation and face it. But he must warn Jackson and Nita and Ram Singh. They would be open to attack, too, as friends and companions of Wentworth. And Dick knew *El Crocodilo* too well to think that the ruthless, power mad criminal would overlook such a chance to strike.

As the cab sped uptown, Wentworth swiftly checked in his mind the weaknesses in his own armor, and the channels through which *El Crocodilo* could best be attacked. The man's invulnerability lay in two things. First, the fact that no one but Don Estéban knew his face. Second, that the purpose of this vicious campaign of destruction was still a mystery. Until Wentworth could learn *El Crocodilo's* ultimate goal, he could not intelligently fight him. But it was impossible to assign a reasonable motive for the wanton destruction of bank after bank.

Wentworth shrugged. Events were moving fast. Before the night was over, there might be other developments which would change the complexion of the entire picture. Perhaps Nita and Ram Singh had uncovered something. If they had, they would be sure to contact Jackson at the apartment, and leave a message.

The immediate necessity now, was to bury Richard Wentworth, temporarily, and assume a new personality through which he could work, unhampered by the police and by the attentions of *El Crocodilo.*

LOOKING OUT of the cab window, he saw that they were just turning on to the Grand Central ramp over Forty-Second Street. This ramp, a testimonial to ingenious engineering, carries traffic directly through the Grand Central Building, into Park Avenue. It would only be a few minutes now, before he reached his destination. The cab radio had been tuned in on WEAF, and subconsciously he had been listening to Fanny Brice as Baby Snooks. Suddenly the program faded out, and an announcer's agitated voice took its place: *"Ladies and gentlemen, with the permission of the sponsors we interrupt this broadcast to bring you an urgent bulletin. The well-known millionaire sportsman and philanthropist, Richard Wentworth, is at this moment a fugitive from the police, charged with concealing information bearing upon the murder of Norton Vandercook. After a thrilling manhunt down Broadway, at the end of which he was believed to have been drowned in a morgue hearse which he drove over the embankment at the Battery, he succeeded in hoodwinking the police, and escaping in the uniform of an aquarium guard. Commissioner Kirkpatrick has issued a general alarm for his apprehension, and has offered a personal reward out of his own pocket, of one thousand dollars. All citizens are requested to be on the lookout for Richard Wentworth. Coming so close on the heels of the astounding series of explosions, murders and suicides, this revelation will be like a bombshell to New York's Four Hundred, among whom Wentworth was considered a respectable member."*

Wentworth grew taut as he suddenly sensed that the cab was slowing up on the ramp. It jarred to a stop, and the driver, who had heard the broadcast clearly, swung out of his seat, gripping a heavy monkey wrench. His face was set grimly as he pulled open the door, brandishing the wrench.

"I thought there was something phony about an aquarium guard grabbing a cab for such a long ride! So you're Wentworth, huh! And there's a thousand bucks reward for you! Will you come quiet, or do I have to knock you out?"

"I'm coming!" Wentworth rasped. He launched himself out through the open door, headfirst. The startled taxi driver swore and tried to swing the wrench, but he was too late. Wentworth's shoulder struck him in the stomach, knocking all the breath out of his body. He went catapulting backward, with Dick on top of him.

Wentworth got swiftly to his feet, and lifted the retching driver up to his feet. The man was green in the gills, and panting for breath.

Wentworth hauled him back into the cab, and laid him on the rear seat, then hastily changed coats and hats with him.

The driver was too weak to offer any resistance, and could not even gasp a protest when Dick removed the man's own belt and strapped his arms behind his back. Then he gagged him with two handkerchiefs tied together, and laid him in the bottom of the cab.

He took out his checkbook and fountain pen, and wrote a check for a thousand dollars. Consulting the license card in its frame, he found that the man's name was John Gamella, and he drew the check to his order, stuck it into his feeble fingers.

"I'm sorry to have to treat you like this," he said kindly. "I realize you must need the thousand dollars pretty badly, so I'm paying it to you anyway, just as if you had captured me. This check is good. I may be a fugitive, but the bank will honor my draft, just the same. And now, if you don't mind, I'll become John Gamella for a little while!"

He left the man, staring dumbly at him from the floor of the cab, and got behind the driver's wheel. He kept the flag down, so that no one would hail him, and drove swiftly off the ramp and up Park Avenue....

Originally, he had intended leaving the cab, and walking two or three blocks to his apartment, to reconnoiter. But now that he was wearing the taxi-driver's uniform, he felt it safe to drive right past the house. He slowed down to a crawl as he passed the building, and his eyes narrowed. The place was certainly being watched—and not by the police!

THERE WAS a car directly opposite the entrance and though he could see it was occupied, it was too dark to make out who was in it. The driver had been careful not to park near a street light. At both corners there were men loitering, and in addition there were other men leaning negligently against the stone wall of the park, on the other side of the street.

Wentworth slowed down, trying to estimate the number of men who were posted here. He counted ten, not including the occupants of the sedan. When he reached the far corner he noted a station wagon similar to the one which had been used to attack the airlines bus. It was parked at the corner, and there was a man at the wheel, but no one visible inside. Of course, it was possible that several more men were hiding, crouching in the body of the station wagon.

He continued past the building without stopping, for he noticed that the driver of the station wagon was watching him. Halfway up the next block, he saw a uniformed policeman. That would be Mike Foley, who had the night beat, and whom Wentworth knew well. It wouldn't do to let Mike get a look at his face. He speeded up just a bit as he passed the patrolman, and then he suddenly stiffened, for he had seen that cop's face under the streetlight, and it was not Foley!

Wentworth knew every cop in this precinct. He faithfully attended all their benefit functions, and called most of them by their first names. But this man who was wearing Mike Foley's uniform was not one of them. He knew it was Foley's uniform, because the numeral—15—shone brightly on the collar under the light.

Grimly, he drove on. *El Crocodilo* had acted with the swift ruthlessness which always characterized him. In order to make sure that he had Wentworth's apartment thoroughly bracketed, he had probably ordered poor Mike Foley killed or knocked out, and had substituted one of his own men on the beat, so that there should be no immediate interference with his watchers.

Wentworth eased the car around the next corner, and made a circuit of the block, turning back into the side street adjoining his house. He had an ace in the hole. That apartment building was owned by him, and he had long ago bought up property in the middle of the block on the side street. He had knocked out the basement walls and built a secret passage to the apartment building. There was a private garage also, in this side street, into which he could drive the cab and leave it.

He slowed up as he approached the garage driveway, and prepared to turn into it. Before doing so he scanned the street on both sides, and uttered a low oath at what he saw. *El Crocodilo* had not neglected even this possibility. There were men here, watching the buildings. And there was another station wagon parked only a few feet from the garage entrance.

El Crocodilo, remembering his previous disastrous clash with the Spider, seven years ago, was not passing up any bets. True, he could not be absolutely certain that Wentworth was the Spider. But he was neglecting no possibilities. The net result of *El Crocodilo's* careful planning was that Wentworth was cut off from reaching his base!

CHAPTER 6
MR. AVERY STEPS OUT

DICK WENTWORTH'S eyes were gray and bleak as he drove on past the garage entrance, and swung south again. He must get to a telephone, and phone the apartment, warn Jackson that the place was covered on all sides.

There was a drug store at the next corner, and as he slowed up to pull in at the curb, his blood began to race. For, looking in the rear vision mirror, he spotted a station wagon tailing him.

It was one of the two that had been parked at the building. Those watchers were nobody's fools. They must have noticed that the cab had circled the block and come back past the side street, and they were following to check on it.

This was indeed relentless pursuit.

Wentworth stopped the cab at the curb. He threw one look in back to make sure that the trussed up taxi driver was not smothering, got out, and entered the drug store. The station wagon pulled up at the curb directly behind the cab, and the driver jumped from behind the wheel. Two other men emerged from the interior. The driver went over to look inside the cab, while the other two followed Wentworth into the store. Almost before they were in the door, guns had appeared in their hands.

Dick had no weapon. And even if he had, he would have been unwilling to risk a gunfight which might attract and injure innocent people as well as attract police. He hurried just a little as he walked down the length of the soda fountain, and called loudly to the soda clerk, "Is there a phone here?"

"In the back," said the clerk.

Wentworth nodded and hurried just a little faster. At the rear, there was a recessed alcove with telephone booths and alongside it a door into the prescription department of the pharmacy. He turned into the alcove, and out of the corner of his eye he glimpsed the two men who had followed him. One was brandishing a gun at the soda clerk to keep him quiet, while the other came toward the rear in leisurely fashion. Convinced that his quarry was going to use the phone, he was taking his time, thinking he had him cornered. Perhaps the fellow figured on overhearing the conversation, and thus making sure of the identity of this cab driver.

But Wentworth did not enter the phone booth. Instead, as soon as he was hidden from sight in the alcove, he stepped through the doorway into the prescription room.

The pharmacist looked up, alarmed, from his prescription table, and Wentworth put a finger to his lips.

"Holdup!" he whispered. "Two men with guns!"

The pharmacist gasped, and applied his eye to the little peephole which permitted him to see into the store. He glimpsed the two men with drawn guns, and his hand began to shake. Wentworth threw a hasty glance around, and saw what he had hoped to find—a back entrance from the prescription room into the side street.

"Stay here," he whispered to the druggist. "I'll go and get help!"

The man nodded, and Wentworth slipped out through the side door. He headed straight back toward the corner where he had parked the cab. When he got around in front he saw that the driver of the station wagon was leaning into the rear of the cab and roughly pulling the gag out of the trussed up driver's mouth.

Wentworth came at him, cat footed. The fellow, alarmed by some sixth sense, swung around and lifted his gun. Wentworth smiled grimly and sliced down with the edge of his hand against the fellow's temple. The blow landed with a *slop* like the sound of a dull axe biting into wet wood. The gunman dropped without uttering a sound.

DICK SWOOPED down and snatched up his gun. He leaned into the cab and found the taxi driver staring up at him, frightened, with the thousand dollar check still clutched in his hand. The gag was out of his mouth.

"I'm going to release you," Wentworth said, "because I don't want those fellows to get you. But if you try anything—"

"Gosh, no, Mr. Wentworth! I wouldn't do anything to harm you—not after you treated me white like this!"

Wentworth nodded grimly, and unstrapped his arms from behind his back.

"Get going!" he ordered.

The driver climbed in front and shifted into first. "God bless you, Mr. Wentworth!" he called back, and then he was gone.

Wentworth swung around and peered into the drug store. One of the men was still keeping the clerk quiet, while the other was tiptoeing to the telephone alcove.

Dick smiled tightly. He ran over to the station wagon and got into the driver's seat. The motor was running, for the gunmen had evidently wanted to be sure of a quick start. Dick put his hand on the horn and blew a shrill blast. He repeated it twice before the gunman near the soda fountain realized it was his own horn, and looked out through the plate glass window.

Wentworth leaned far out and waved tauntingly to the fellow.

The chap shouted something to his partner in the rear, and leaped for the door, but before he got to it Wentworth was feeding gas into the motor and racing away. He had kept his promise of getting the gunmen out of the drug store. He turned the next corner just as two shots cracked out behind him, and then he was speeding west, free of pursuit.

Now he had a little breathing space. Those gunmen would surely not report the theft of their station wagon to the police. But *El Crocodilo* would certainly inaugurate a still-hunt for Wentworth now.

The station wagon was a nice, roomy car, with a smooth, powerful motor. Wentworth drove it all the way over to the river, and then proceeded to examine it. With an army of thugs as well-organized as this one, they would need a headquarters and supply depot. Perhaps something in the car would give him a clue to the whereabouts of that headquarters.

In the driver's cab there was a sawed-off shotgun on the floor, and a small submachine gun on the seat. Inside, there was a selection of revolvers and rifles, and a bag full of grenades. The collection of lethal weapons suggested that it was designed to accommodate a considerable number of men. How many of these station wagons *El Crocodilo* had at his disposal, Wentworth could not guess. But they were an effective means of transporting armed units to any projected operation.

Of a clue, however, there was no hint.

Wentworth got out and looked at the license plates. They were so obscured by mud that he had to wipe them off in order to read the number. As he had expected, they were of no help, for they were of the "0" series—a series reserved for taxicabs. These plates had probably been stolen, and it would be no use tracing them.

Dick left the station wagon and crossed the street to a cigar store. He entered the booth and dialed the number of his residence.

"Jackson!" he said.

His faithful man's voice came over the wire, speaking carefully, and stiltedly.

"Mr. Wentworth is not in at the moment, sir. Who is this calling?"

Dick's eyes gleamed. He understood that Jackson was trying to convey one of two things to him—either there was someone in the apartment at his elbow, or else the phone was tapped.

"This is Mr. Rayburn," he said, subtly altering his voice.

"Ah, yes. Mr. Rayburn! The gentleman who was interested in selling the Club Mexico! Mr. Wentworth should be back in *two* or *three* hours, sir. But I shouldn't advise you to call tonight."

WENTWORTH GRIPPED the phone tightly. Jackson's reference to the Club Mexico was obscure. He knew of the place, but had certainly never been interested in it. The only connection he could get out of it was that perhaps Nita or Ram Singh had phoned in earlier, and named that place for him to meet them.

As for the *two* or *three* hours, that was a definite, prearranged signal. Two, mentioned pointedly meant that the police were present. Three, meant that other enemies were present. Then Jackson knew that the apartment building was bracketed by *El Crocodilo's* men, but they were on the outside. It must be the police, then, who were in the apartment. Kirkpatrick must have sent them over at once, to wait for him in case he attempted to return. It had been a good thing, then, that *El Crocodilo's* watchers, below, had prevented him from going up!

He had all the information he could get under the circumstances, and now it was only necessary to close the conversation without arousing suspicion, if possible. He was aware that if the police were in the apartment, they would also have tapped his wire, and that this call was being traced as a matter of routine. No doubt a radio car was slipping up here at this very moment.

"Thank you, Jackson," he said. "I shall get in touch with you again. Goodbye."

He hung up and stepped quickly out of the phone booth.

The radio above the cigar counter was tuned in on a news broadcast, and the proprietor was listening to it with rapt attention: *"To take our minds off the European conflict, it appears that we are developing a moody little war of our own, right here in New York. As a climax to a series of murders and mysterious explosions in banks, Norton Vandercook was stabbed to death tonight on the eve of making an important revelation to his Board of Directors, and the First Avenue State Bank was destroyed by another of those half ton demolition bombs. In this connection, police are seeking Richard Wentworth for questioning, and Commissioner Kirkpatrick's personal offer of a thousand dollar reward has been increased at an emergency meeting of the city council, to five thousand dollars."*

Wentworth heard this as he passed through the store to the door. He looked out into the street, and saw the headlights of a car speeding down the avenue toward him, about three blocks away. He couldn't tell what kind of car it was, but the odds were strong that it was the police.

He darted across the street, and got under the wheel of the station wagon, and got it moving. Since he was heading in the direction from which the approaching car was coming, he would have to pass it. It was only a block away now, and he was able to distinguish the white top and green body of a police radio car. They were coming for him, all right!

He didn't know whether the cops had seen him cross the street. If they had, they'd surely stop him. His hands gripped the wheel hard as the police car raced abreast of him, and his foot was ready to push all the way down on the accelerator if they should hail him.

But they didn't. They concentrated all their attention on the house numbers. He heard the screech of their tires as they pulled up in front of the cigar store, and ran in.

Grimly he turned the corner, and headed across town. The cigar store owner would give them a description of the man who had phoned, and they would know that Wentworth was no longer attired in the aquarium guard's uniform. He had to secure a change of costume, and get to the Club Mexico as quickly as possible. If the police had acted this fast on the tapped telephone wire, they would also think of investigating the Club Mexico.

FORTUNATELY, HE had always maintained several emergency retreats scattered about the city, where he kept complete changes of outfit, disguise material, and equipment. He drove directly to one of these, on the east side, only a block away from a police station house. It had always been his policy to select spots for emergency headquarters in busy sections, and in close proximity to the police. For instance, he had one place in an old office, across the street from police headquarters, and another opposite the Criminal Courts Building. Very often it was necessary for the Spider to have a place which afforded quick refuge and at the same time permitted him to observe the actions of the police. These places served that purpose, and at the same time were not subject to suspicion. It was the same in the case of this East Side hideout. The police never suspected that the Spider would hole up only a block away from a precinct house.

Wentworth parked the station wagon squarely in front of the station house. He was reluctant to part with it, but he couldn't afford to retain any connection between Wentworth and the new personality he was about to assume. At the same time, he felt that the authorities might glean valuable knowledge from a study of the machine. He swiftly block printed a note.

"To the Police:

This station wagon was used by thugs in the employ of *El Crocodilo.* I suggest that you dust it for fingerprints, and try to trace the source of the weapons. If you will raid the block around the apartment house of Richard Wentworth with a large enough detail of men you will pick up a dozen or so of *El Crocodilo's* men, and another station wagon like this one. My regards to Commissioner Kirkpatrick, and tell him not to allow his blood pressure to go too high. Assure him that my friend, Richard Wentworth, is still alive, but that I have decided he is not clever enough to cope with *El Crocodilo.* I have decided, therefore, to take over, and I am putting Wentworth on ice for a while, to keep him out of danger.

Believe me to be,

Sincerely yours,

The Spider."

He placed the Spider seal on the paper alongside the signature, and wrapped the note around the steering wheel, after carefully wiping finger prints from the wheel, the shift lever and the door handle. Then he got out and walked away, nonchalantly.

In a few moments he was upstairs, in a third floor apartment of one of the better class buildings in the neighborhood. This apartment was rented in the name of Ronald Avery, supposedly an archaeologist who was doing special research work before forming another expedition to Egypt. The natural explanation of his long absences was that he had to make protracted trips to museums all over the country to compare antiquarian objects. But nobody bothered to inquire into his business, and the landlord was certainly not one to initiate inquiries, since, by some strange coincidence, the building was owned by the socialite, Richard Wentworth!

ONCE IN the apartment, Wentworth drew down the Venetian blinds, and turned on a special calcium light, which shone directly over the dressing table. He stripped off the clothes he had worn, and dropped them down the incinerator, then seated himself before the mirror.

His fingers moved with all the dexterous swiftness of the skilled makeup artist as he applied pigment and facial tone creams to his face, neck, and chest. Out of compartments in the dressing table he brought special plastic material, aluminum bridges to fit over teeth, cunningly wrought nostril plates to change the shape of his nose, and gum wads which aided to increase the breadth of his jaw.

While he worked, he had the radio going. It wasn't necessary to search around the dial for news. Every station was carrying special broadcasts. Sam Slattery, the I.B.C.'s ace newscaster, was on the air. Slattery had an inside track as a crime news reporter for one of the great Metropolitan dailies, and he had often scooped the whole country on some of the Spider's exploits. The Spider had often given Slattery advance information, and in return for this, Slattery had carried on a steady campaign, in the newspaper and over the radio, in favor of the Spider.

Tonight, Sam Slattery's broadcast was particularly edifying: "*... while I admit that I haven't been in touch with the s, I am sure that he has interested himself in this case, which has the whole city in a state of panic. In the first place, there's the incident in Queens tonight, where the Spider fought six unidentified gunmen, single-handed, and snatched an unknown victim from the point of death. The police haven't played this up very strongly. Why not? Because they won't admit that the Spider has beaten them to the punch! Ladies and gentlemen, I tell you sincerely that, while Commissioner Kirkpatrick* *wastes his time offering rewards for a man like Richard Wentworth, there is a far greater criminal among us. Have any of you heard of EL CROCODILO? No! Because the police have kept that name a dark secret from the public! They haven't told you about the little crocodile medallion found on the murderer of Norton Vandercook! They haven't told you that all six men killed by the Spider in that gunfight in Queens also carried those medallions! All they told you was that the Spider killed them. Well, if you want to know more, ASK COMMISSIONER KIRKPATRICK ABOUT EL CROCODILO!"*

Slattery's rich voice paused for a moment, and then he finished: *"Ladies and gentlemen, my time is up. And that's about all I have to tell you now—except for one thing more. Somewhere in this city, the Spider is working, quietly and efficiently, to spike the guns of EL CROCODILO. It's a war between the Spider and EL CROCODILO, with the police merely acting as dazed onlookers. My advice is, if the Spider should ask any citizen for help, GIVE IT TO HIM. The Spider is your friend, and mine! Goodnight and God bless you all!"*

WENTWORTH SMILED under his makeup. "Good old Sam," he murmured. He left the dressing table, and crossed to a telephone concealed behind a false bookcase. He dialed the number of the I.B.C. radio station, and asked for Slattery. When he got him, he said, "This is Mr. One." He heard a sudden intake of breath at the other end. Slattery had no idea who the Spider was, but when he got a call from Mr. One, he knew that he was being given a scoop.

"I advise you," Wentworth hurried on, "to be at the Club

Mexico within twenty minutes." Then he added in a lower voice, "And thanks for the kind words!"

He hung up, smiling, without giving Slattery a chance to thank him, or to ask a question. Then he quickly finished disguising himself. When he was through, he gave himself a final, last minute inspection in the mirror. He was changed through and through, even to the expression of the eyes. To all intents and purposes, there stood here a florid, heavily-jowled, dark-haired man of about forty, with a high-scholarly forehead and a pair of shell rimmed glasses. He had two gold teeth in the upper jaw, and a small, well-waxed moustache. Though his shoulders were broad and powerful, he appeared to be a little heavy in the waist. The use of cunningly applied plastic material gave the impression of high cheekbones. The modest tweed suit with the padded shoulders was designed effectually to conceal the presence of two heavy automatics in shoulder clips, and a well hidden pocket in the flaring back of the jacket held the Spider's cape and hat.

Wentworth nodded in satisfaction. Here then, was Professor Ronald Avery, archaeologist and world traveler!

He left the apartment house boldly, and hailed a cab.

"Er—I should like to go—er—to the Club Mexico," he told the driver hesitantly.

As they passed the police station house, he smiled a little secret smile, for he saw the precinct captain and a group of bewildered policemen clustered around the parked station wagon, and reading the note from the Spider! He wished he could hear their remarks.

CHAPTER 7
THE CROCODILE SNAPS HIS JAWS

ON THE way to the Club Mexico, they crossed Park Avenue, and on a sudden swift impulse, Wentworth—alias Ronald Avery—tapped on the window and instructed the driver to stop off at the Vandercook residence.

He had suddenly remembered a frail little old lady with pure gray hair, who had patted his arm.

What was she doing tonight? Was she still holding her head up under the double impact of her daughter's abduction and her husband's death? Even though Nita might need him at the Club Mexico, if he could but say a single word to that frail old lady, a word which might help her to keep her shoulders straight, it would be well worth the loss of time.

The doorman at the Vandercook house didn't recognize him, of course. He instructed the man to phone up and say that Mr. Ronald Avery was calling, at the request of a friend. She immediately asked him to come up.

Mrs. Delia Vandercook was alone in that great, cold penthouse apartment. Even the butler was gone. And there were no reporters, no visitors. In the stress of weird events which had been crowding one another today, the widow of the murdered banker was forgotten. She had been downtown to look at her husband's body, and then they had sent her home, because they were going to perform an autopsy on him.

There were dark rings under her eyes, and her gentle, kindly face was unnaturally flushed. It was evident to Wentworth at first glance that only a frantic and desperate anxiety about Ellen was keeping her on her feet. Yet she managed a wan smile at the door, and said, "Come in, Mr. Avery. You said that you were sent by a friend?"

"Yes, Mrs. Vandercook," he told her, carefully disguising his voice. "Mr. Wentworth asked me to stop in. It is impossible for him to call in person, due to his unpopularity with the police. He asked me to assure you that he has not forgotten about your daughter, and that he is devoting all his energies to finding her. He says that you are not to give up hope until you hear from him definitely to the contrary."

Delia Vandercook stood facing him in that same familiar attitude in which he had seen her yesterday—with one hand at her breast, her head high. Her eyes were on him, keenly, appraisingly.

And a thing now happened, which had never happened to Wentworth before. So startling was it, that he almost lost his composure. Mrs. Vandercook suddenly smiled a kindly and tender smile, and a glint appeared in her eyes.

Very clearly and very distinctly she said, "My dear Dick Wentworth! I think it's wonderful of you to come here to reassure me, with the police hunting you all over the city!"

For a moment, Wentworth was speechless. Never had a disguise of his been pierced—even when subjected to the suspicious scrutiny of trained man hunters. No actor had ever attained his skill in makeup, and in the use of disguising mannerisms. Yet this little old lady had torn the mask from him after a single appraising glance!

She came forward impulsively, and put a hand on his arm.

"You *are* Dick Wentworth, aren't you?" she asked softly.

He nodded. What was the use of trying to bluster it out? He couldn't look into those clear, sorrowful eyes, and lie.

"How in the world did you know, Mrs. Vandercook?" he demanded. "Have I made a mistake? Did I give myself away?"

"No, no, Dick. No one would ever know you. I—I wasn't even sure, myself, until you admitted it. But there was something deep down in your eyes that seemed to be talking to me with another voice. Perhaps it was the sympathy, and," her voice broke just a little, "the pity you felt for me."

SHE FORCED a smile. "And then there was something else. You had given your word that you would not speak of Ellen to a soul. Yet you wanted me to believe that you had broken your

word by sending a stranger with a message about her. I know you, Dick. I know how good your word is."

"Thank you," he said. "I had to come. To tell you how sorry I am—about Mr. Vandercook. I was only a few minutes too late."

"I know. I know." She turned her back upon him abruptly, and he heard a stifled sob. Then she dabbed at her eyes with a tiny handkerchief, and faced him.

"Oh, Dick, what about Ellen? Norton is dead. I—I must face that fact. But—I'm afraid I haven't the courage to sit and wait for news of—Ellen's death...."

"You must keep your head up, the way you always have. If it's humanly possible, I'll save her."

"You—you have a lead? A clue?"

He bowed his head. "I'm sorry. You're not one I can deceive. I have only an intangible clue. I'll follow it up, though. It may lead me to *El Crocodilo.* If I can get to him, I'll get Ellen back for you."

"You, Dick? You alone against *El Crocodilo?* Your disguise is excellent. But what chance would you have, without experience in crime, standing against *El Crocodilo?*"

He could see in her eyes, and hear in her voice, that what she wanted was some reason for hoping. Some thread to hang her courage on.

"It's not I, alone, Mrs. Vandercook," he said gently. "I—have a friend. A friend who can help a great deal. The—Spider!"

He saw her tauten as he spoke the name. A flicker of light raced across her face. She sobbed a great, glad sob, and suddenly she buried her face against his shoulder. "Oh, Dick, I know it now! I see it all! What a fool I've been, thinking you a wealthy idler! It's *you!* You're the Spider!"

"Please, Mrs. Vandercook! You mustn't jump to conclusions—"

"You needn't worry, Dick! Your secret is as safe with me as if I were your mother. And you needn't tell me whether I've guessed right. I *know.* And I'm glad—glad that you're the Spider, because now, Ellen has a chance... If only Norton were alive to know this!"

Gently, he disengaged her hands, and led her to a chair.

She was weary with the reaction from her sudden burst of emotion, but she still held her head up.

"Au revoir, Mrs. Vandercook," Richard Wentworth said softly. And then, under his breath, not knowing whether she heard it or not, "The Spider salutes you!"

He went quietly from the room.

His cab was waiting downstairs, and in fifteen minutes he alighted in front of the Club Mexico. An orchestra was playing inside, and the strains of an unenthusiastic rumba floated out. The Club Mexico was a second-rate night club, and they did not encourage casual patrons. It seemed that they had a pretty steady clientele of Latin Americans. The doorman looked without favor at the ruddy, Nordic face of the new arrival.

Wentworth, paying off the cab at the curb, cast a quick glance up and down the street. The first thing he saw was his own limousine, parked a few feet down. Ram Singh was standing disconsolately near it, and two or three men were loitering nearby. The chances were good that those men were agents of *El Crocodilo.* It would never do for Wentworth to approach Ram Singh and talk to him, for that would immediately draw the attention of the watchers to him.

Ram Singh had seen him, though. The Sikh was familiar with the personality of Ronald Avery. He moved a few feet from the limousine, toward the entrance of the club.

WENTWORTH WAITED a moment, until his cab had pulled away. Then he did an artistic stagger, at the curb, a good imitation of a gentleman who has had just a bit too much to drink. He staggered a little more, and collided with Ram Singh.

"Whyncha watch where y're goin'!" he barked.

"Pig!" said Ram Singh. "Thou art an unbeliever. Thou art drunk!"

"Izzat so!" shouted Wentworth. "I'll show you!"

He took a wild swing at Ram Singh, and missed by a mile. Then he closed in, and clinched with him. The two of them struggled at close quarters, wrapping arms around each other, and getting their heads close together. Wentworth's right ear was in Ram Singh's beard, and the Sikh whispered, "Master, I am watched!"

"I see that. Where's Miss Nita?"

"Inside. We followed the man that snatched paper, and he came here, but the swine knows who we are. I fear for Mistress Nita, yet she will not permit me to remain beside her. She watches the man who took the paper, yet she knows that she too is being watched!"

Their awkward struggle had attracted a small crowd, and several hands were pulling them apart. They could talk no more, so Wentworth abruptly let go of Ram Singh's neck, and stumbled around wildly. He voiced loud and dire threats, and Ram Singh sniffed with contempt and walked back to the limousine.

Wentworth grumbled, and went into the Club Mexico. The doorman thawed out considerably when he was handed a ten dollar tip.

Inside, he spotted Nita at once. She was sitting at a table near the left wall, with a glass of wine in front of her. She saw him at once, but she gave no sign of recognition. There were some two dozen couples on the dance floor, mostly Latin Americans. The band was making more noise than music, but the customers seemed to like it.

Wentworth saw Sam Slattery at another table, close to the bandstand. He stood unsteadily between two tables till the head waiter came over. He gave him a ten dollar bill, peeling it from a seemingly inexhaustible supply, and loudly demanded a table near the wall, close to Nita's.

The headwaiter, seeing his wad of money, was glad to oblige. Wentworth allowed himself to be seated, and called for champagne.

He turned around and stared insolently at the people seated at the nearby tables, and in this way he sized them all up. One man with a bright green necktie was sitting morosely and hugging a highball glass, about two tables away, near a door marked. "Lounge." At another table two other men were talking in low voices.

Wentworth hiccoughed, and lurched in his chair, almost falling out of it. He put a hand on the floor to support himself, and palmed a wadded bit of paper which Nita had flipped over. It was a sheet of cleansing tissue, and Nita had written in lipstick: *"Two men watching me. Believe they are waiting for you to contact me. Man with green necktie is one I followed. He has gone upstairs twice. Private rooms above, and some sort of meeting is going on in one of them. This place gives me creeps."*

Dick refrained from smiling. He picked up a book of matches, lit one, and applied it to the rolled up tissue. Then he waved it like a torch, and yelled, "Hooray for the Yanks!"

Patrons at the other tables looked at him with tolerant amusement, and the waiter bringing his champagne looked pained.

"Where's the men's room?" Dick demanded.

"Right through that door, sir."

DICK PUSHED up to his feet, and wove toward the door. He went through it into a corridor, with a men's lounge on the right, and a ladies' dressing room on the left. At the far end of the corridor there was a staircase. He mounted swiftly to the upper floor. Here there were six private rooms. He listened at the door of two of them, and heard nothing. But from the third room there came the drone of voices.

He moved down the hall, and tried the next door. It was unlocked, and he stepped inside. There was no light in this room. He stood for a second at the door, waiting to be sure there was no one lurking here, and then he shut the door softly and went to the window. It opened on a narrow ledge, overlooking an alley.

Wentworth busied himself for a minute, withdrawing various objects from his clothing. Among other things, he had a thin plastic mask upon which was a clever replica of the noto-

There were two automatics in his hand... "Good evening, gentlemen," he said.

rious face of the Spider. He spread this over his face, fastening it behind his head. Then, the black cape and low brimmed hat completed the conversion. The dark and shadowy figure which seemed to ooze over the windowsill and onto the ledge might have been part of the night.

In a moment he was alongside the window of the next room. The blind was pulled all the way down, but the window had been left open a crack at the bottom. The Spider crouched on the ledge, and gently pushed the blind inward, so that he could see under it.

The room inside was filled with men—eight or nine of them. Three he recognized at once. They were the death merchants, Schmidt, Roganov and Niti. He knew most of the others, too. They were all men whose names appeared on the list furnished by Don Estéban, many of whom Wentworth had talked with yesterday. The bankers were seated in chairs along one wall, while the three death merchants sat facing them, at a little table upon which was spread writing material. Roganov was talking.

"So you see, my frien's, that those who will not do business with us come to no good end. It iss better to take our terms. *El Crocodilo* becomes impatient. Would you have him treat you as 'e 'as treated Power, an' Boyce, an' Vandercook?"

One of the bankers, Arthur Backer by name, leaned forward in his chair, trembling with emotion.

"Damn you! Damn the three of you! You've practically admitted that you're hand in glove with *El Crocodilo*. All we have to do is notify the police!"

Roganov smiled tolerantly, and threw a humorous side-glance at Niti and Schmidt.

"That iss correct. You 'ave only to notify the police, Meestaire Backer. An' w'at of your eleven year old son? W'at will 'appen to heem?"

Backer groaned, and shut his eyes. He slumped in his chair.

Roganov nodded. "You all understand, no? You must do the business wit' us." His glance became arrogant, strayed along the row of nervous bankers. "You, Simmons, mus' worry about your daughter. You, Flemming, about your twin sister. You others—do you wish your dear ones to suffer? *El Crocodilo* is one without mercy to those who oppose 'im."

Those five businessmen were silent.

Crouching at the window, the Spider's face was grim and hard.

ROGANOV WENT on, talking smoothly. "We three are but fiscal agents of *El Crocodilo.* We 'andle the cash transactions. An' after all, it is not much that we ask. True, you mus' sell us controlling stock in your banks. But we pay—in cash. You lose nothing. You will still be rich men."

Percy Simmons, the head of the Coast Trust Company, asked doubtfully, "And what if we agree? When—when will we see—our loved ones again?"

"Vair-ee soon. W'en you agree, they will be released from the shackles, but will be kept in custody for a few days longer—till *El Crocodilo* has obtained full control of American finances. Through control of your banks, we can spread our influence to the whole country. Then we will be so powerful that we will not care if you go to the police. Then your loved ones will be released. But you mus' give your answer now. The papers are ready to sign. There," he waved his hand toward a trunk in one corner, "is five million dollars in currency—enough to pay you all."

"What about me?" asked another banker, named Stoner. "You've made me do other things—got me in a financial jam. Even selling my stock won't get me out of it. When they investigate my bank—"

Roganov smiled, and raised a hand. "That will be taken care of, Stoner. They cannot investigate a bank which has been destroyed—by a demolition bomb!"

There was a gasp from the other men. "That's why those other banks have been destroyed!"

"But naturally. We empty out the currency an' then destroy the building."

There was a long silence in the room. The bankers looked at each other, doubtfully. At last Flemming said, "Well, we have no choice. As long as they're paying us in cash for our stock, I say—let's sell."

The others nodded in agreement.

Roganov rubbed his hands. He shuffled the papers on the table, and then nodded to Schmidt, who went to the trunk and unlocked it. He began taking out packages of currency.

At this moment the Spider chose to make his entrance.

He pulled up the shade, and stepped into the room. There were two automatics in his hands, and the black cape billowed out about him.

"Good evening, gentlemen!" he said.

Eight pairs of eyes stared at him in horrid fascination, wavering between the two grim automatics, and the terrible, glittering eyes that glinted under the hat brim. There was not a man in the room who did not know who this was. There was not a man in the room who did not feel a cold finger of terror.

"The Spider!" gasped Percy Simmons.

ROGANOV AND Niti sat as if transfixed. Schmidt stood near the trunk, with his hands full of money, never moving.

The Spider did not look at those three. He spoke to the five bankers.

"Gentlemen, there is something you should know, before you close this deal. I don't blame you for what you're doing. No man should be censured for making a sacrifice in behalf of those he loves. But *this* sacrifice is too great, even for that. Vandercook made it. He is dead. Power and Masters and Boyce made it. They are dead. You, too, will find that death is sweeter than life—if you close this deal!"

"What—what do you mean, Spider?" Hemming demanded.

"I mean that you are being hoodwinked. The money which you are being paid for your stock is counterfeit. Vandercook found that out. And he was in no position to complain, for just as in your case, his daughter was still a prisoner of *El Crocodilo.* He had sold his stock—but he couldn't spend the money he had received for it. So he chose to die. But he was killed before he could commit suicide, because he had written a letter, explaining about the counterfeit money. *El Crocodilo* couldn't afford to let that become public, so he ordered Vandercook killed. The letter was taken. Tonight, it was brought here, and given to one of these three vultures."

He swung toward Roganov, Schmidt and Niti, "Which one of you has it?"

Schmidt blurted, "I know nothing—"

But Lawrence Stoner exclaimed, "That's right! A man with a green necktie brought a paper up, and gave it to Roganov!"

The Spider's bleak eyes swung to the Russian. "Hand it over!"

Roganov wet his lips with his tongue. He glanced sideways at his unholy confreres, and then looked once more into the Spider's eyes. He put a hand in his pocket and brought out a folded sheet of paper.

"Lay it face up on the desk!"

He obeyed.

The eyes of the five bankers gravitated toward it, and they read the lines which Vandercook had pecked out on his typewriter that evening. A stunned silence filled the room.

"And now, gentlemen," the Spider went on, "you can see how much faith to put in the words of these vultures. You can see how much chance there is that they will release the hostages in *El Crocodilo's* hands!"

Flemming groaned. "What—what are we to do? If we notify the police, the Crocodile will surely kill our loved ones—"

"I suggest, gentlemen, that you place this matter entirely in my hands."

Some of these men had heard Sam Slattery's broadcast, earlier in the evening. They were inclined to trust the Spider. It was Flemming who spoke for all of them.

"What of my sister? What of Simmons' daughter? What of the others that *El Crocodilo* is holding? Can you save them?"

"I don't know," the Spider told them. "I can only try."

"That's good enough for me, Spider!" Simmons exclaimed. "I place myself in your hands!"

"I, too!" echoed Stoner.

One after another, the others followed suit.

The Spider inclined his head. "Thank you, gentlemen. And now, please truss up these three criminals as thoroughly as you can. Use their belts, and do a good job!"

THERE WAS a look of savage satisfaction in the faces of the five bankers as they swarmed over Roganov, Schmidt and Niti. They didn't worry about being gentle.

Only Backer was worried. "What will *El Crocodilo* do when he finds out about this? He may kill all his hostages—"

The Spider nodded grimly. "We must find out where they're being held—and quickly!"

He looked down speculatively at the three bound men, "Perhaps one of you would wish to talk?"

They all glared up at him with defiant hatred.

The Spider turned to the bankers. "Have any of you ever been permitted to visit the hostages?"

"Yes!" exclaimed Flemming. "They take us one at a time. It's my turn to visit my sister tonight. That man in the green necktie is the one who takes us. He's waiting for me, now!"

"I see!" the Spider said softly. "Then you shall go, Flemming!"

"But—but what can I do, alone?"

"You will not be alone!"

"Ah!" exclaimed Flemming. "You will follow?"

"Yes. How do you go?"

"We go in a car, out into the country. They put heavy goggles on us, with glass that you can't see through, and side blinders. Somewhere in the country, we get out of the car, and take a train. They explained, the last time I went, that I was a blind man being taken home. The ride in the train lasts an hour, and then we get in a station wagon. The goggles aren't taken off until we're in a room with blank walls, and a barred window."

Flemming's voice broke. "That—that's where I talked to my little son, the last time. He—he was shackled to the wall!"

The Spider's eyes glittered. "Wait ten minutes, after I leave, then go downstairs and tell the man with the green necktie that you are ready. Try to act natural, and above all don't look around to see if you're followed. It may give your guide ideas which he shouldn't have."

Suddenly, the other four bankers all spoke as if moved by a common impulse.

"Spider! Let us go, too!"

Simmons put out an appealing hand. "It's our sons and daughters and sisters whose lives are at stake. We have a right to take the same risks that you take. Let us follow Flemming, along with you!"

The Spider studied these men quizzically. They had been weak, and ready to yield to pressure. Some of them had engaged in sharp business methods. But they were human, and they loved their families. They deserved a chance to fight for them.

"All right!" he said softly. "You may come. And there's one

other trouper who will also want to come along!" He stepped to the telephone, made sure it was not a private branch exchange, and dialed the number of the Vandercook home.

"Mrs. Vandercook? This is… a friend you saw once tonight. We're getting up a little expedition. Do you want to come along and help strike a blow for the right?"

"Oh, yes! Yes!" she breathed. "It will be better than sitting here."

"Get in a cab, then. Be at the corner opposite the Club Mexico, in less than ten minutes!"

He hung up, and turned to the others. "We'll leave Roganov, Schmidt and Niti here for the police to find. With that trunk full of counterfeit money, they'll have a good deal of explaining to do!"

As he spoke, he was tearing down the drapes from the window, and twisting them into a rope. He tied one end to the radiator, and hung the improvised rope out of the window.

"All right, Simmons, Stoner, Backer, Mason! Climb down to the alley, one at a time. Don't go out the front way. Work your way to the back street, and wait to be picked up at the corner. When you see me next, I'll be a florid faced gentleman with a small moustache and a wide nose!"

HE WAITED till the last of them was down, and then turned to Flemming. "Exactly ten minutes after I leave here, go down and tell the man with the green necktie that you're ready!"

"I understand!" said Flemming, with shining eyes.

The Spider bowed mockingly to Roganov, Schmidt and Niti, and backed out of the window. In a moment he was back in the next room, and had shed the Spider disguise. He encountered no one on his way downstairs, but when he opened the door a crack to peer into the main dining room, he became taut. Nita was no longer at her table. The two men who had been watching her were also gone, but the possessor of the green necktie was still there.

Wentworth felt a cold shiver of apprehension. Nita would not have gone away now, unless under compulsion. Could it be…?

His worst fears were realized as he staggered past her vacant table, once more in the role of the tipsy gentleman. A small medallion lay on the white tablecloth—a medallion bearing the bas-relief figure of a crocodile, with a naked girl in its slavering jaws. And scrawled in black crayon on the cloth were the words: "For the Spider!"

He did not touch the medallion. Though his blood was racing, he gave no sign of having noticed the absence of Nita, or of the medallion.

He called loudly for his check, and then wove his way out, unsteadily.

He had hoped that Ram Singh would not be outside, for that would have meant that Nita had gone away voluntarily with him. But the Sikh was there, and that dashed Wentworth's last hope. He knew now that he was in the same position as Flemming and Simmons, and those others. He, too, must go to seek a loved one at an unknown destination.

He must work swiftly, now. And he must take long chances.

Abruptly, his mask of tipsiness left him. He made no pretense of not recognizing Ram Singh, but walked boldly up to the limousine.

The Sikh, seeing his new attitude, grinned broadly in his beard, and opened the door for him, then got behind the wheel, ready for orders.

"Listen carefully, Ram Singh!" Wentworth said swiftly. "Miss Nita is in the hands of *El Crocodilo.* I need a conveyance and weapons for at least four other men. We have no time to seek for such a thing. We shall try to have the enemy supply us. Do you understand?"

"I understand, Master!" the Sikh said, grinning eagerly. "The pigs shall accommodate us!"

He started the limousine with a spurt, and shot up the street.

Looking back through the window, Wentworth nodded in satisfaction. As he had hoped, one of the two station wagons parked near the club had started in pursuit of them.

"So far, so good, Ram Singh!" he said through the speaking tube.

CHAPTER 8
THE DEVIL'S PRIVATE CAR

RAM SINGH drove two blocks, and then slowed down so as not to lose the pursuing station wagon. He made a right turn, without instructions from Wentworth, and drove steadily for three blocks.

So well did these two—master and man—work together, that it was unnecessary for Wentworth to give further instructions.

In a few words he had outlined the situation, and his need. To have said more would have been to insult the intelligence of the proud Sikh. Another block and Ram Singh saw what he was looking for. It was a short, dark street just off the riverfront, which would be utterly deserted at this time of night.

With the station wagon a block behind he made a sharp left turn into this street, and then clamped on his brakes. The powerful Daimler stopped as if it had hit a stone wall.

Wentworth, who had known just what Ram Singh intended, was braced for the shock. Almost at the same moment that it stopped, he was out of the car, and crouching alongside it with both guns in his hands.

The station wagon came streaking around the curb, on two wheels, and for an instant the driver's terrified face was visible as he realized that his quarry had stopped short directly in his path. He twisted the wheel desperately, frantically, in an effort to avoid hitting the Daimler, at the same time stepping on his brake.

Before he had come to a complete stop, Wentworth was at his side. The driver uttered a startled squawk, and reached for a revolver on the seat at his side. At the same time, two more gunmen came barging out of the side door of the station wagon.

Wentworth laughed a deep, booming peal of laughter. He took two steps back, and both of his guns began to blaze in synchronized, death dealing time. The driver slumped over the wheel, with his head virtually blasted off, while the two gunmen were smashed backward against the station wagon, with bullets through their hearts.

By the time Ram Singh came running over, there was nothing further to do.

The Sikh lent a hand, and they dragged the dead driver out from behind the wheel. They laid the three bodies in a row on the ground, and Wentworth took an additional minute to impress the Spider seal on their foreheads, leaving them there for the entire world to know that three more servants of crime had paid the supreme penalty to the Spider's avenging guns.

Wentworth peered into the interior of the station wagon and

nodded with satisfaction. It contained the same complement of lethal weapons as *El Crocodilo's* other cars: sawed-off shotguns, a submachine gun, revolvers, and grenades. There would be enough here to arm his improvised corps of volunteers. He got behind the wheel, and issued swift instructions to Ram Singh.

"Follow me, keeping a hundred feet behind at all times. I will be following a car which will leave the Club Mexico. If, for any reason, I should be prevented from continuing the trail, you will take over. We must not lose that car, Ram Singh. It may mean the lives of many innocent people—including that of Miss Nita!"

"Never fear, Master!" Ram Singh said. "We shall not lose them!"

Wentworth turned the station wagon around, and drove back to the Club Mexico, with the Daimler trailing him. By his watch, only eight minutes had elapsed since he had left the Club. He was just in time for his rendezvous.

SURE ENOUGH, Stoner, Backer, Mason and Simmons were waiting at the corner. When they saw the station wagon pull up, they gave way to momentary panic thinking it was one of *El Crocodilo's* vehicles.

Not until Wentworth spoke to them in the voice of the Spider could they bring themselves to understand the coup which their leader had executed. They piled in with grim eagerness, and selected weapons from the supply in the interior.

Watching the look on their faces, Wentworth could imagine that they would make good use of those weapons tonight.

A moment later, Mrs. Delia Vandercook arrived in a taxicab.

She was breathless with excitement, and her pathetic eagerness at the prospect of actually being able to help in the search for her daughter brought a lump to Wentworth's throat. He assigned her to ride in the Daimler with Ram Singh.

Hardly had these arrangements been completed, when Wentworth, at the wheel of the station wagon, tensed at the sight of two men who had just emerged from the Club Mexico. One of them was Flemming. The other was the man with the green necktie. Flemming was wearing a pair of the goggles which he had described. Green Necktie guided him by the arm to the curb, where they stood, apparently waiting to be picked up.

Almost at once, a car appeared in the street and purred to a silent stop in front of the Club.

Wentworth's eyes narrowed when he identified it as a private ambulance—one of the long, sleek, streamlined kind that are in use these days by so many private hospitals.

Green Necktie turned and motioned to someone inside the club, and two men appeared, carrying a stretcher between them. A shrouded figure lay on the stretcher, covered with a sheet from head to foot.

Wentworth felt his blood racing as he watched them load that stretcher into the ambulance. It was Nita—of that he was sure. They were taking her away to *El Crocodilo's* headquarters to be held with the other hostages. She must be either drugged, or securely bound and gagged, for he had been able to detect no sign of movement from the figure on the stretcher.

Involuntarily, his hand stole toward his shoulder holster. To step out of the station wagon and blast his way to Nita's side was his first and most natural instinct. Any other man would have done just that. Richard Wentworth, the man, would have done so. But he was more than Richard Wentworth. He was—the Spider—and his obligation was not alone to Richard Wentworth and Nita van Sloan, but to those others who had placed their faith in him, and who trusted that he would lead them to the rescue of those they loved. He must let Nita go in that ambulance, he must let her face whatever menace arose, in order that others might be saved.

As soon as the stretcher was in the ambulance, the two men who had carried it returned to the Club Mexico, and Green Necktie pushed Flemming up the steps into the interior. He closed the door behind them, and the chauffeur sent the long, sleek ambulance hurrying away on its ride of destiny.

With every sense alert, Wentworth drove the station wagon in its wake, with Ram Singh following at a hundred feet.

Wentworth dared not pull up too close, lest he be noticed. And he dared not trail too far behind, lest he lose the quarry.

THE TRAIL led up into the outskirts of the city, and then across on a wide parkway. The miles clicked off, one after another, with monotonous regularity. They turned off the parkway and followed a macadam road for a while, then swung into a state highway. They passed through several small towns, and at last as they approached another, the ambulance slowed down and turned off toward the railroad station.

Wentworth, following, switched off his lights, and drove in the wake of the ambulance's tail light. Ram Singh did the same. The station proved to be a minor junction where engines were switched. A luxurious private car stood alone, on a siding. The ambulance stopped beside it.

The driver came around and assisted Green Necktie to carry the stretcher into the railroad car; then Green Necktie led Flemming aboard. The driver of the ambulance pulled it over into the parking space, and then returned to the private car.

Wentworth, watching at a distance of a hundred feet from behind the wheel of the station wagon, heard Stoner and the others whisper excitedly behind him.

In a few moments, a short passenger train pulled into the junction, and the private car was coupled on to it.

"All right," said Wentworth. "Let's go." Moving swiftly in the darkness, he made for the train, followed by his small army. Mrs Vandercook and Ram Singh brought up the rear.

"Disperse all through the train," he told them, "so as not to attract too much attention. Keep your eye on that private car. When they get off, we must get off too."

Five minutes later, the train rumbled out of the station. When the conductor came through to collect fares, Wentworth learned that it was an Albany local. The private car, he learned, belonged to a certain Hans Schmidt. Beyond that, he could learn nothing. Not knowing how long he would remain on the train, he bought a ticket to the end of the line. Two or three of his volunteers were in the same car, while the others occupied the two cars ahead. Up at the front, just behind the mail coach, was the private car. It had been coupled into the middle of the train because the mail car had been coupled in at the same time.

The steel wheels clicked a continuous clattering dirge as

the train rumbled steadily northward, stopping at each small station. Wentworth wondered what was happening to Nita in that private car. At last, he could contain himself no longer. He got up and went forward.

When he reached the platform of the private car, he tried the door cautiously and found it locked. The train was slowing up for a crossing, and as the rumble died down. Wentworth heard a sound from inside that car, which made his blood pound furiously. It was a cry of pain.

Now he hesitated no longer. He sprang up on the iron rail, and hauled himself to the roof of the car. The train began to move swiftly once more, and the wind tugged at him with fierce plucking fingers as he crawled forward. At the middle of the car, he gripped one of the side rails of the roof, and swung over the side, hanging on by one hand. This brought him far enough down so that he could see into the windows. Clinging precariously against the mighty pull of the wind, he felt the hot blood pound in his veins. They had taken the shroud off Nita in there. Obviously, they had been questioning her. Green Necktie had hold of both her hands, which were twisted behind her back, while the ambulance driver was playfully flicking the sharp point of a gleaming knife toward her eyes.

EVEN AS he looked, Wentworth saw the ambulance driver switch his attentions from Nita's eyes to her cheek. He gripped her hand in one hand; and started to draw the edge of the knife down along her cheek.

Wentworth drew back his foot, and smashed the window in.

Both men whirled in startled surprise, and a gun appeared in Green Necktie's hand.

From his perch outside the car, Wentworth fired only twice. His first bullet smashed into the stomach of Green Necktie, and his second took the knifeman square in the forehead.

Nita sprang up, uttering a glad cry. "Dick!"

"Open the door for me!" Wentworth shouted against the wind.

She nodded her understanding, and he drew himself up to the roof once more and climbed back to the platform.

Nita was waiting for him with the door open.

"Dick!" she said. "I hoped you were following! But you should have waited. They would have taken us to the others!"

Wentworth took her in his arms. "I couldn't hang on there, and watch that maniac slice you up!"

They returned into the car. Flemming, who had been out of sight from the window, came running over, tearing the goggles from his eyes. "Good God," he exclaimed, "I heard what they were doing to Miss van Sloan. But I dared not interfere!"

"That's all right," Dick said.

He knelt beside the two men he had shot. The ambulance driver was dead. Dick's eyes narrowed as he inspected that man's face. Here was no Indo-European, or even an Asiatic. That narrow head, with the high cheekbones and the bronzed skin, and the black straight hair could belong only to a Yucatan Indian, or perhaps to one of the descendants of the Inca tribes. This, then, must be one of the Indian knifemen whom *El Croc-*

odilo had imported from South America. He turned away from this one, to look at Green Necktie.

Green Necktie was not dead. But his stomach wound was draining the life from him at a rate appallingly fast. He lay upon his back with the terror of death in his eyes, and both hands clapped to his stomach. A weak tremor of sound pulsed from his quivering lips.

"Doctor… get me… doctor…."

Wentworth knelt beside him without touching him, without a flicker of compassion in his face.

"Where were you taking Mr. Flemming and Miss van Sloan?" he asked coldly.

"Get… doctor…."

"You'll get no doctor till you talk. You'll die right here on the train!"

The abject fear which shone in that man's eyes was something almost unclean to behold.

"I'll talk… only… get… doctor!"

"Where is *El Crocodilo* holding his hostages?"

"At Hudson Heights… near… river…."

The man's voice trailed away into a dry rattle. Blood flecked his lips. He stiffened in a spasm of agony, and then fell limp. He was dead.

Bleak-eyed, Wentworth came to his feet.

"Hudson Heights!" he exclaimed. "That's the next station! Flemming! Go through the train and tell the others!"

CHAPTER 9
LAIR OF THE CROCODILE

ONCE FLEMMING had gone, Nita van Sloan faced Wentworth, flushed and excited. Her beauty was enhanced a thousand fold by the color that had come flooding her cheeks.

"Dick! What are we going to do? From what these men said, I gathered that this train will be met by another ambulance, driven by someone named Tito, who will take us to *El Crocodilo's* headquarters. But now—this Tito will know the truth. He won't take us there!"

"We'll make him talk!" Wentworth said harshly.

"Suppose—suppose he's stubborn? These men said he's one of those South American Indians, completely dominated by *El Crocodilo.* He may be willing to die, rather than betray his master!"

"Then we'll search every bit of the countryside around Hudson Heights."

She shook her head. "If Tito doesn't return with the ambulance, *El Crocodilo* will know something has gone wrong. He—he may kill all his hostages!"

She came close to him, and put a hand on his sleeve.

"Don't you see, Dick? You have no right to take a single chance with the lives of those poor prisoners of *El Crocodilo's.* Hemming and Simmons, and the others, trust you. You can't let them down. We must make *sure* that this Tito leads us to the headquarters!"

"What do you want to do?" Wentworth demanded, hoarsely. He knew very well what Nita wanted to do, yet he hated to face the fact that it must be done.

"You've got to let me go on as a prisoner. You can make up sufficiently like this dead man, to pass for him in the dark. You'll have to fool Tito into thinking everything is all right."

He nodded slowly. "We'll do it, Nita. Go tell Ram Singh to keep the others out for five minutes."

Eagerly, she went to the door, and he heard her whispering to the Sikh, and the Sikh's rumbling voice in answer. In the meantime, he knelt beside the dead man, and spread out his makeup kit and mirror on the seat beside him. Swiftly, his skilled fingers removed the makeup already on his face. They flew, as he applied other plastic material, pigments and lotions. There were only a few minutes now before the train would arrive at Hudson Heights. In that short time he must perform a miracle of artistry.

Timing himself, he found it was only four and a half minutes when he finally rose to his feet, and took a last look in the mirror. As a finishing touch, he had taken the dead man's green necktie. In the dark, he stood a good chance of passing for him. He hoped that he would not have to exchange many words with Tito. Once inside the ambulance with Nita and Flemming, he need only wait until they arrived at the secret headquarters of *El Crocodilo.*

At a signal from him, Nita allowed the others to enter. Swiftly he explained to them what he planned. Flemming must put on the colored glasses once more, but with some of the coloring rubbed off, so that he could see a little through them. He gave each of them a gun. The plan was, that as soon as they arrived at the station, they should leave the train by the last car, which would be far enough removed from this one so that Tito, the driver of the ambulance, would not see them.

Ram Singh would then hurry to the parking lot which always adjoins a country railroad station, and would "borrow" one of the parked cars. He did not explain to them that Ram Singh carried master keys which would open the ignition of virtually any car made.

"What then?" demanded Stoner.

"Then," Wentworth said, "you will follow the ambulance at a respectable distance. Give the driver no opportunity to guess that he is followed. And trust to God that Tito will lead you to the place where your loved ones are being held. Once there, you will wait outside until you hear shooting. Then you'll charge!"

He turned to Delia Vandercook. "As for you—"

She showed him a gun, which she took from her handbag.

"I'm going right along!" she said with conviction.

Wentworth might have tried to argue with her, but the train began to slow down for Hudson Heights. Hurriedly, he sent them scurrying out to the last car. Then Nita lay down on the stretcher and he covered her with the shroud, but he did not tie her hands and feet. She kept the revolver stuck in the front of her dress.

WENTWORTH TOOK one last look in the mirror, and shrugged. He hadn't attained as perfect a likeness of the dead gunman he was about to impersonate, but he had managed to suggest enough similarity so that anyone expecting to see that man might be fooled. To make more certain, he went through the car, unscrewing most of the electric light bulbs. In the dimmer light, he was more satisfied.

He turned to Flemming, and asked anxiously, "Do you think I'll pass?"

Flemming was more optimistic than Wentworth He nodded enthusiastically. "It's marvelous, Spider! I don't see how you do it! With you in charge, we can't fail!"

Heartened somewhat by Flemming's confidence, he went to the door just as the train came to a jarring stop at a dimly lit, lonely wayside station. Opening the door and stepping out on the platform, Wentworth saw a sleek, streamlined ambulance pulled up just inside the loading gate. A long-haired Indio came toward the train, peering up at him.

"Tito?" Wentworth asked, speaking in a whisper. He had not heard Green Necktie talk, except when he was dying, and he had no way of knowing what his normal voice sounded like. Therefore, he spoke in a sort of hoarse whisper.

The Indio grunted. "Where Niki?"

Wentworth assumed that Niki was the knifeman he had shot, who had been threatening Nita with the dagger.

"Niki not come," he said. "You must help with stretcher."

He had brought the stretcher out on the car platform with the help of Flemming, as he didn't want Tito coming inside the car and seeing the dead bodies. He first guided Flemming down onto the station, and then Tito took one end of the stretcher while he took the other. They carried it quickly to the ambulance, and then Wentworth sped back to the private car. The conductor was waiting there, and Wentworth nodded to him that it was all right to go ahead.

The conductor waved his lantern as a signal to the engineer, and then climbed up on the platform of the next car after the private one.

"Orders are to uncouple your car at Albany and leave it there to be picked up on the down trip of number eighty-six, tomorrow. Is that correct, sir?"

"Okay," Wentworth said.

He stood there while the train pulled out. Out of the comer of his eye he had seen the figures of Ram Singh and the others descending from the last car, and disappearing into the darkness. He was perfectly satisfied that the private car should ride to Albany with its dead freight aboard. The longer it took before those bodies were discovered, the better he would like it.

As soon as the train was gone, he took Flemming's arm and helped him along to the ambulance. Though Flemming could see quite well out of his goggles now, they still had to maintain the impression that he could see nothing. Flemming climbed into the interior of the ambulance and sat down alongside Nita's stretcher. Wentworth, with his hat pulled low over his face, was about to enter, too, but Tito, who had come around to the rear, stopped him.

"You no come, Lukens. *El Crocodilo* say you take next train back New York. Train come in ten minutes. You go see Schmidt, quick."

Wentworth's blood went cold. He had not counted on this. To

let Nita go into the stronghold of *El Crocodilo,* with only Flemming along, was more than he had bargained for.

"I'm coming with you," he said. "I've got to see *El Crocodilo* about something—"

"You no come!" Tito said stolidly. "You got orders. You do what orders says!"

He slammed shut the ambulance doors, and fastened them with a padlock. Then he went around in front, and got behind the wheel.

Wentworth followed him. "I tell you, I got to see the Boss—"

Tito looked down at him queerly. "You crazy? Wen *El Crocodilo* say, *do this*—you do! Take train. Goo'bye!"

He backed the ambulance up, and started to turn it around.

FOR AN instant Wentworth was desperately tempted to shoot the coldblooded Indio, right on the spot. He couldn't stand the idea of having Nita carried away in that locked ambulance, without him. But then he thought of the others. At the other end of the station, he saw a car without lights, moving slowly along. Ram Singh had found a car, and they were just waiting for the ambulance to leave, before following it. But if he stopped Tito from driving away now, those others would have no trail to follow. They would be cut off from the ones they loved. Wentworth had no right to place Nita's safety above that of anyone else.

He sighed, and bowed his head. "Okay, Tito. You going right back to the place?"

"Sure I go right back. Where else you t'ink I go?"

Tito leaned over the side of the car, and gave him a searching look. "What the matter with you tonight, Lukens? You sick?"

It was fortunate that it was dark. With his face so close to Wentworth's, Tito would surely have discovered the deception if there had been more illumination.

"No," said Wentworth. "Just nervous."

"You better look out," Tito warned. "*El Crocodilo* no like his men be nervous. He get rid quick of nervous men!"

The Indio showed his teeth in a malevolent grin, and patted a knife which was stuck in his waistband. Then he made a significant gesture with a forefinger across his throat, and winked.

Wentworth held himself in check. He did not move until Tito had tooled the ambulance out into the road. Then he broke into a run and raced diagonally across the platform toward the slowly moving bulk of the car which Ram Singh had purloined. He got out in the road, and Ram Singh slowed down for him.

With an eye to accommodating the small army which he had to transport, the Sikh had not selected a sedan, but had chosen a small, half ton open truck, belonging to some vegetable dealer, whose name was inscribed on the side. If that truck were damaged tonight, the owner would be surprised to receive a letter in the mail, containing a sum of money sufficient to replace it with a much more costly vehicle.

The five bankers were crouched in the body, straining their eyes to watch the disappearing tail lights of the ambulance. Delia Vandercook was seated in the cab, alongside of Ram Singh, and she moved over to make room for Wentworth who leaped on board while it was still in motion.

Swiftly, Wentworth explained why he had not accompanied the ambulance. "Don't lose them, Ram Singh!" he urged huskily.

The Sikh gave him a grim nod. His big hands were clamped hard on the wheel, and his eyes held the road ahead, where the twin red lights joggled along at an increasingly swifter pace. Ram Singh knew what an effort it had cost his master to let Nita go in that ambulance. Delia Vandercook also knew, and she pressed his hand in the darkness murmuring, "God bless you forever, Dick Wentworth!"

But those in the back could not guess what was passing in the mind of the Spider. Though they knew who Nita van Sloan was, they had no idea that the Spider was the man who loved her—no whit less than they loved those poor hostages whom they hoped tonight to save. Knowing that Nita was affianced to Richard Wentworth, they accepted Ram Singh's presence here, for they were aware that he was in Wentworth's service.

DRIVING WITHOUT lights, Ram Singh managed efficiently by keeping his eyes on the white line in the middle of the road, while Wentworth and Mrs. Vandercook watched the tail lights of the ambulance. Twice, Wentworth had to urge the Sikh to go faster, lest they lose the ambulance. Once he cautioned him to slow down, for the ambulance had reduced its speed, and they were coming too close.

"They're heading over toward the river," Wentworth said at last. "It can't be far, now!"

At the river, the ambulance turned north, and followed a narrow two-lane road that ran under the lee of almost vertical cliffs on the right. The river bank was only a few yards away.

Mrs. Vandercook sat with both hands in her lap, clasping and unclasping them nervously. Now that they were nearing the crisis, she found it almost impossible to maintain the attitude of fortitude which Wentworth had so admired, before.

"What—what if *El Crocodilo* has already killed Ellen?" she asked huskily. "I—I couldn't bear it...."

"Wah!" exclaimed Ram Singh. "If he has killed her, I will break the pig's neck with my own hands!"

She smiled wanly in the dark at the fiery Sikh's threat. It was hardly a comfort to her, but she felt Ram Singh's sympathy, and could not but react to it.

Suddenly, Wentworth exclaimed, "Look sharp, Ram Singh! They're turning off!"

The road branched here, one fork continuing along the river, and the other going off at an angle. The ambulance took the fork that led inland. Slowing down just enough to keep the distance between them, Ram Singh turned off, too. A hundred yards further, the ambulance came to a full stop, and Ram Singh had to stand on the brake to keep from pulling almost abreast of them. They were so near that they could hear Tito, the driver, calling to someone.

His hail was answered, and he swung the ambulance in toward a driveway, which was barred by a heavy iron gate. Now, they could see that the whole length of the estate down here was fenced in, with wires running along the fence. It must be electrically charged.

A man standing at the gate with a rifle under his arm had answered Tito's hail. He turned a flashlight on Tito's face, and only after doing that did he press a button inside the gate. Almost at once, the heavy gate began to swing open, and the ambulance drove in. The gate swung shut after it.

"It's controlled from the house!" Wentworth said. "The only way that gate can be opened, is by signaling an operator at the house!"

They watched the ambulance climb the steep driveway up toward the building at the top of the cliff. When it was half way up, a powerful floodlight on the roof of the structure burst into being, and limned the ambulance.

Wentworth, watching keenly, saw it pull up under a portico, saw Tito come and unlock the door at the back, and Flemming come out, feeling his way as if still unable to see. Then men came from the house and carried the stretcher in, with Nita on it.

The floodlight went out, and everything was dark.

Almost at once, a dreadful sound arose from up there—the baying of bloodhounds. Then shrill, keening cries rose into the night, weird and bloodcurdling.

Mrs. Vandercook shuddered. "How in the world can we get in there?"

Simmons, Backer and the others in the rear of the truck crowded forward.

"Good Lord," exclaimed Backer, "what'll we do? We can't storm the place. And if we call the police, *El Crocodilo* will surely kill every soul up there. He—he said that's what he would do if we made trouble!"

Backer looked at the high fence, and groaned. "God in

heaven, Spider, do something! You got us to defy *El Crocodilo.* You promised you'd help—"

Wentworth had been studying the high cliff with a thoughtful eye.

"There must be a back way in there," he said to Ram Singh, speculatively. "We'll have a look."

HE TURNED to the bankers. "Ram Singh and I will take the truck around to the river road, and try to reach the house that way. It may be that Miss van Sloan will find a way to let us in, before she's overpowered. You four will remain here, facing the gate. You're all armed. If you hear shooting up there, and if the gate opens, then you'll know that Ram Singh or I will have reached the house. Come up on the run."

"Suppose we hear shooting," Simmons asked, "and the gate *doesn't* open?"

"Then," Wentworth told him grimly, "you better get the police. Ram Singh and I won't be alive to help you any longer!"

The four bankers descended from the truck, and crouched in the darkness. Delia Vandercook remained in the truck.

"I want to see how the Spider works!" she announced.

Ram Singh brandished a high-powered Mannlicher rifle, which he had carried on the train from the Daimler, concealed in a fishing rod case. "This will come in handy, Spider!"

He held the rifle between his knees, and backed the truck up, then turned around and retraced their course to the river road.

The back of the estate faced directly along that road, overlooking the river. Here too, there was a fence, strung with electrified wire. Inside the fence, they could see thick underbrush everywhere. The grounds were not kept clean and neat, but had been allowed to grow wild. Wentworth kept peering in through the fence as they drove up the road, seeking for a possible path to the top.

But they traversed the whole distance of the fence, without his having been able to find it.

"There must be a path in there!" he said. "I'll have to go in and look!"

He had Ram Singh drive the truck up close against the fence. It was still some six feet above the level of the truck, and if he should touch one of the electrified wires at the top, it would certainly ring an alarm signal up at the house.

"Master," said Ram Singh, "it cannot be done. There is no way to reach that house by surprise."

"I think there is, Ram Singh. Come. Climb in the back with me!"

In the back of the truck, he grasped the sideboards, and found that they were set in the floor on pegs, so that they could be taken out. Soon, he and Ram Singh had them all out, except for one at the end, next to the tail board. He laid the other boards diagonally across the tops of these, and then stood on them. The boards came to almost two feet of the top of the fence. A three-foot high jump would carry him over the top, to land on the weed covered grounds inside.

Ram Singh grinned. "It is good. Let me go first, Master—"

Wentworth shook his head. "I'm going alone, Ram Singh. There are dogs on the grounds. If they should attack me, you'll have to cover me with the rifle. And you can't cover me if the dogs are attacking you, too. So you stay *outside,* with the rifle. If you hear the dogs, then swing the truck around and turn on the headlights so you can see how to shoot!"

The Sikh grumbled in his beard, but did not argue.

Delia Vandercook came in back, and took Wentworth's hand. She pressed it against her cheek, her kindly old eyes brimming with tears.

"God keep you safe, Dick. I know you're doing this for Ellen and the others as much as for Nita. God bless you!"

Dick patted her cheek. Then he tested the boards, flexing his knees for the jump.

"Here goes!" he said, and leaped high into the air.

His jump carried him clear of the fence, with plenty of room to spare. He twisted gracefully, like an expert high jumper, and landed on his feet in the soft underbrush.

"I'm going to work my way down along the fence," he whispered to Ram Singh, "and look for a path. Follow me with the truck."

Then he started off.

CHAPTER 10
ODDS AGAINST THE SPIDER!

NITA VAN SLOAN lay motionless beneath the sheet as her stretcher was carried into a long hallway. She had taken the revolver out of her blouse, and placed it under her, and she had also taken the precaution of putting both her hands behind her back, as if they were still tied.

In a moment, she was glad that she had done so, for she heard a brusque command and the stretcher bearers stopped. A voice spoke in crude Spanish which she understood only with difficulty. But she caught enough of the meaning to cause a dreadful thrill of terror to run through her. That brusque voice said, *"Watch her carefully. She is not tied, and she is armed!"*

"Sí, sí, El Crocodilo!" answered one of the bearers, in the same odd Spanish dialect.

"The Spider, and others, is outside. We must trap them!" the voice of *El Crocodilo* hurried on.

Nita's blood congealed when she heard that. How could *El Crocodilo* know this? How could *El Crocodilo* know that she was untied and armed? How could he know that the Spider was outside?

There was only one possible answer, and she had it now, as the sheet was ripped from her. She swung lithely to her feet at the same instant, twisting around and raising the revolver. Her guess was correct. Bertram Flemming stood there, minus his goggles. There was a satanic look of hatred in his eyes as he glared at her, while two of his Indios tried to grab her aims.

Flemming! It had been Flemming all the time! Posing as a victim with the others, he had been able to influence their decisions. He would have succeeded in getting them to agree to the terms laid down by Roganov and his co-merchants of death, had it not been for the appearance of the Spider at that moment, in the room above the Club Mexico. Then, seeing that the Spider had the upper hand, he had conceived the idea of luring the Spider right into his headquarters. It would be a simple matter now for him to phone back to the Club Mexico and have his three emissaries freed.

All this Nita saw in a flash as the two Indios came at her. She started to raise her gun to shoot *El Crocodilo* to death, but she didn't have the chance. The Indios were upon her, and she had to defend herself. She fired twice in such quick succession that the shots sounded almost as one. The two Indios fell into her, for their forward momentum carried them on, but they were both dead before then bodies touched her.

Nita sidestepped deftly, twisted clear of the death sprawling bodies, and turned for a shot at *El Crocodilo.* But he was gone. He had stepped behind a doorway, and his voice, raised in imperious summons, was calling for assistance. He apparently had no wish to chance a shot from Nita's gun.

At his command, the hall was filled with black-haired hulking Indios who charged in at Nita with knives in their hands. They held their knives by the blades, ready to throw. One of them hurled his weapon, and Nita fired. She hit him in the chest, and the knife flashed over her head. The other knifemen were closing in with terrible swiftness, and she counted more than a dozen. It would be impossible to kill them all.

SHE FIRED twice more, downing the two foremost, and that stopped them for a moment. She turned and ran down the hall, zigzagging to avoid the thrown blades which whizzed past her. There was a bend in the hall, and she turned into it. She stopped short, losing all hope. Several more Indios were coming toward her down this hall. There was no escape.

Around the bend in the hall she heard *El Crocodilo's* voice,

urging his men on. She couldn't turn back. One swift glance as she came into this bend had showed her that there were doors down its entire length, all with bars across them. This, then, would be where the prisoners were kept.

Desperately, she raised the bar of the nearest door, and thrust it open. She leaped inside just as a knife skimmed past the back of her neck. An Indio leaped at her, and she shot, and the man screamed and fell almost at the threshold. She slammed the door shut, and leaned against it, breathlessly. There was no way to lock it from the inside, but it was heavy oak and they would not be able to penetrate it either with knives or guns. If only she could find some way of locking it!

Strangely enough, the Indios were not trying to force their way in. She heard a murmur of voices outside, and decided they were holding a council of war. They knew she still had a couple of shots left in the gun, and were trying to devise a means of getting her without risk.

Suddenly she was startled by the sound of movement inside the pitch-dark room. She jerked her gun up, and then uttered a little gasp of pity. A frail girl was moving across the room, and chains clanked as she walked. Nita looked at her with eyes that were becoming accustomed to the dark, and said, "Oh, you poor thing!"

"Who—who are you?" asked the girl.

"I'm a friend. There are others here, trying to save you. But—but I'm afraid *El Crocodilo* will get us before they can come up."

"Oh," said the frail girl. "I—I'd given up hope of ever being saved. I'm Ellen Vandercook. They've had me chained here for days and days. I'm not chained to the wall, but they've put shackles on my legs, and look—they've tied my hands behind my back. *El Crocodilo* is a monster. See that window, high up there? He's left it open and unbarred. I can look at it all day and all night, and know that if I could get up there, I could escape. But—but I'm tied, so I can't climb—even if I could reach it. The men come and jeer at me, and pretend that they'll untie me so I can escape. And then—laugh at me!"

Nita's eyes had grown narrow as she heard Ellen speak. She looked up at the window, and saw that it was truly unbarred and open.

"Come here, quickly, Ellen. While they're thinking what to do, I'll untie you—"

"You can't, I'm handcuffed—"

"Oh!" Nita swallowed hard. "Listen, Ellen. If I boost you up, will you take a chance and jump from the window? It's your only chance."

"I'll do it! I'll do it! Only—if you move away from the door, they'll come in—"

She stopped, sucking in her breath, as the voice of Bertram Flemming—alias *El Crocodilo*—came to them through the door.

"Miss van Sloan! Can you hear me?"

"Yes, I can hear you," said Nita. "Why don't you come in after me," she taunted.

El Crocodilo chuckled. "All in good time, Miss van Sloan. I won't have to lose any more men to get you. I'm setting a little trap for your friend, the Spider. I'm opening the gate down below, and he will surely come up, with his ridiculous volunteers. As soon as they reach the house, I shall set off a demolition bomb. That will very thoroughly take care of all of you. You, Miss van Sloan, are being locked in here. I just thought I'd tell you about it, so that you can anticipate a very pleasant death."

NITA FELT the trembling body of Ellen Vandercook close beside her. Then she heard a scraping sound outside, as the bar was set in place.

"My men and I will be well on our way to safety by the time the Spider gets up here!" she heard *El Crocodilo* say.

While he talked, she pushed Ellen Vandercook over to the window. "Come! I'll boost you up—"

"But what about you? You can't reach the window by yourself. You'll be locked in here when the bomb goes off—"

"Never mind! Your job is to run as fast as you can, and find the Spider down by the gate—or somewhere on the grounds. Warn him about the demolition bomb. And above everything, tell him that *El Crocodilo* is—Bertram Flemming!" She cupped her hands, and made Ellen place a bare foot in them.

"Go down the back way, toward the river," she whispered hastily. "If I know anything of the Spider, he'll be around there, looking for a means of getting in. Quick now, no argument," as Ellen made a protest, "your mother is waiting down there for you!"

She boosted her up to the window.

"If—if anything happens to me," Nita said steadily, looking up, "tell Dick Wentworth that—that I—love him!"

And then she gave Ellen a shove and sent her up through the window. She heard a thud on the other side, and held her breath. Then she heard a scrambling in the underbrush. Ellen was running.

Grimly, Nita turned away from the window. There was no use looking up there. She couldn't reach it, no matter how she tried, and she had little hope that Wentworth could get here before the bomb went off. But at least she had sent little Ellen Vandercook back to her mother. Dick Wentworth would have done it that way....

Suddenly Nita stiffened, uttered a muted groan of despair. From outside she heard the voice of one of the Indios raised in excitement, and then a thrashing in the underbrush out there, as of a big man running. At the same time, the voice of *El Crocodilo* was raised in urgent command. Nita closed her eyes in despair. Ellen's escape had been discovered. She was being pursued. Shackled as she was, she could never outrun that Indio.

Nita's shoulders sagged. She closed her eyes and leaned against the wall....

OUT IN the darkness, Ellen Vandercook stumbled through the underbrush frantic with terror. From close at hand came the baying of hounds, held in leash. If they were released, she would be torn to shreds. She ran, stumbling, and the thorns plucked at her flimsy dress, trying to rip it from her.

The shackles about her ankles hindered her, and the handcuffs that bound her wrists behind her did not even permit her to swing her arms. She fell down half a dozen times in two minutes, constantly pushing up to her feet, remembering the words of Nita van Sloan. She must get down there, not so much for her own sake, as for the sake of Nita and of the other prisoners up in the bleak house. She must warn the Spider—must warn the Spider—must warn the Spider... The words began to whirl about in her mind like a colored pinwheel as she ran and stumbled, ran and stumbled.

Suddenly she heard shouts behind, and threw a frightened glance up the hill. She spied the lumbering form of an Indio, and a scream welled up in her throat, and died there. He was racing after her with long legged strides that ate up the distance between them.

"Oh, God!" she moaned.

She turned and stumbled on, her hobble clanking at her bare feet, which were already bloody and torn from the loose stones and gravel in the path. She fell, and her impetus carried her rolling down the hill for a way, her body gashing and bruising itself. That hulking shape behind drew ever closer, silent and ominous.

She tried to struggle to her feet, and only reached her knees. Every last fiber of her was straining to carry her forward, urged by the frantic instinct of self-preservation, but she could go no further. She lacked the strength to push herself up upon her bleeding feet.

And now it was too late. That great hulking shape was looming over her. In the night it seemed to be some ugly gnome of darkness, with twisted ungainly limbs and strangely grotesque head. In its right hand it held a knife, long and curving to a point, with an edge that was honed to razor sharpness. Its left hand reached out and seized a fistful of the yellow ringlets atop the unfortunate girl's head. Then the blade swept around, with the hungry edge questing for her throat.

"No, no!" screamed the girl, "Don't kill me!"

The Indio held her thus for a moment, with the knife poised. In the gloom of night which encompassed them, it might have appeared that he was merely prolonging the act of murder. He held her thus for a moment, and turned to look up toward the house.

Almost at once, the searchlight on the roof sprang into life again. Its long, darting finger seemed to feel tentatively along the hillside until it found them, and then it settled, bathing them in eerie luminance. The Indio stared straight up into the light, his eyes narrowed almost to pinpoints. Then, the searchlight went out, as abruptly as it had appeared.

The Indio kept watching the house, as if for a signal. A light appeared at one of the windows. It flashed on and off three times, then disappeared.

The Indio grunted. *"El Crocodilo* says—*to kill!"*

He lifted her savagely by the hair, and drew back the knife for a slashing blow at her throat.

And it was at that moment that a harsh voice came to them: "Stop! Stop, I say!" It was the voice of the Spider!

HE WAS racing up the hill toward them. It had not taken him long to find the path down there, and the searchlight from the house had shown him the girl and the Indio. But he dared not shoot, for the darkness made shooting inaccurate, and Ellen was between himself and the Indio. So he shouted—with the desperate hope of staying that knife.

The Indio saw the gun—and the Spider's grim countenance. He bared his teeth, and spat like an infuriated tiger. He raised his head and gave voice to a long, keening cry such as one might hear in the dense jungles of the Amazon basin lands. That ululating cry went rippling up the hillside, and almost at once the searchlight on the roof of the big house flared into brilliance once more. It picked them out unerringly, limning Wentworth's lithe body as he continued to race the twenty yards which still separated him from the Indio and the girl.

The light blinded the Spider, but he kept going anyway, shielding his eyes with one hand, and holding his gun ready for the first good chance he might get to shoot.

But *El Crocodilo* must have prepared for every contingency, for hardly had the Spider taken a dozen more steps, then there sounded the sharp and snapping crack of a high-powered rifle. The bullet screamed overhead, and struck the bough of a maple tree, chipping off a strip of bark.

The tough maple bark snapped downward as if it had been shot from a catapult, and struck Wentworth's right wrist. The shock numbed his hand momentarily, and the gun dropped from his nerveless fingers.

The Indio saw that, and uttered a screech of triumph. He threw Ellen down upon her face on the ground, and leaped straight at the Spider, with his knife upraised. He uttered a weirdly chilling cry, and drove down with the knife, straight at Wentworth's heart.

The Spider's reaction was that of the trained fighting man. To dodge that driving knifepoint was impossible; to take it in the heart was death. There was only one alternative. His left hand snaked up and caught the naked blade!

The weapon cut through the palm of his hand, gashing it to the bone. But his clenched hand slid down the length of the blade, stopping against the hilt. In spite of the biting sharpness of the wound, he kept his fist clenched around the steel, and thrust out against it, pushing the point back from his chest.

The whole weight of the Indio was behind the driving weapon, and the only thing that kept it from striking into the Spider's heart was the tension of his arm.

Thus the two combatants stood locked, almost toe to toe, while the glaring searchlight bathed them both in its merciless brilliance. The Spider's grotesque face betrayed no inkling of the terrible tension upon his left arm. But the knifeman's simian features were contorted into a horrid mask of baffled rage. The Spider laughed his hollow, taunting laugh and twisted hard to the left, so that his elbow pushed against the Indio's side. The thrust sent the simian faced man over to one side, and his forward straining body did the rest. He pitched forward on his face in the path. The Spider had released his painful hold upon the knifeblade, and he now held his hand palm up to lessen the flow of blood. He stood in the glare of the searchlight, his ominous, black cloak billowing out on the night wind. He was apparently careless of the fact that there was a marksman up at the house, with a high-powered rifle. It was not carelessness, however. For, out of the corner of his eye, he had seen Ellen Vandercook push up to her feet, and start to take a stumbling step down the path, right into the beam of light. If that marksman up there was going to shoot again, the Spider wanted to draw his attention away from the girl.

He shouted to her, "Get back, Ellen—"

But she ran toward him, shouting something incoherent, and did the worst thing possible—she stepped right into the line of fire from the house.

HE CURSED under his breath, and flung himself toward her. He caught her about the waist and fairly dragged her off her feet, into the underbrush, and out of that merciless searchlight glare. Almost simultaneously, there was the wicked crack of the rifle, and a bullet sang through the air, embedded itself in a tree trunk.

Ellen was sobbing against his shoulder as he dragged her further into the scrub, while the searchlight swiveled, in search of them. At the same time, he looked around for the Indio. The knifeman was nowhere in sight. Either he had escaped back to the house, or else he was hiding close by.

"Get down low, and keep quiet," the Spider whispered. "If that searchlight finds us, the rifleman won't miss again!"

"You are—the Spider?"

"Yes."

"Nita van Sloan saved me. She—she's a prisoner in my cell. She helped me get out. *El Crocodilo* is going to set a time demolition bomb, and destroy everybody up there. In God's name Spider, your work is just beginning!"

The Spider's eyes suddenly went bleak. Nita van Sloan locked in a cell up there! He had no time to think of that, for the searchlight was moving inexorably toward them. He drew Ellen farther back, behind a tree. And then, with startling suddenness, the searchlight was doused in blackness!

Impenetrable darkness blotted everything except for the lights in the house at the top of the hill.

Ellen was saying, "Nita said to tell you—Bertram Flemming is *El Crocodilo*—"

What she said barely registered on his mind, for just then, he heard another sound which brought a muttered oath to his lips. That sound was the sudden, furious baying of bloodhounds.

The baying grew louder, and there was a thrashing in the underbrush. *El Crocodilo* was playing another ace. If he could not lure the Spider up there, he was at least going to try to catch him with bloodhounds. The beasts had already scented their prey, and they were converging upon them. And suddenly, the first of the great brown beasts burst from cover, into the path. There were a dozen of them, their sleek coats glistening in the dark, then eyes like flickering points of fire.

They ceased baying. Low growls rumbled in their throats. They were coming in fanwise as the Spider stood up to face them, with Ellen cowering behind him. His other automatic was in his left hand, but he knew how hopeless this would be. He might shoot four, or five, or six. But the others would come in to tear him and Ellen apart with their powerful fangs.

He smiled grimly. Here was death, and he could smile—as Nita was probably smiling, up there in the house.

"Go!" he said to Ellen, over his shoulder. "Hobble down to the road—" And then the leading beasts were leaping at him, with slavering fangs! His gun came up, and he fired automatically, straight into their faces. Again and again he fired, knowing even as he did so that it was a hopeless fight, and expecting every moment to feel fangs ripping his throat.

Yet, strangely enough, none of the vicious beasts reached him. For a split-second he wondered about that, and then he knew the reason why. For, above the thunder of his own heavy automatic, he heard the sharp and spiteful crack of the Mannlicher rifle behind him, in the hands of Ram Singh.

IT WAS all over in a moment. The last of the beasts jerked spasmodically on the ground, and then Ram Singh was at his side with a *whoop*....

The Spider turned and saw another sight that brought a lump to his throat. Behind Ram Singh, Mrs. Vandercook had come laboring up the hill, with a gun in her hand, her face set with the resolve not to shirk in the effort to save her daughter. But when she saw Ellen, shackled and frightened, she dropped the gun and uttered a broken cry. "Ellen!"

Her arms encircled the girl, as they both sobbed.

The Spider had time for only a single glance at mother and daughter. Even if he had had ample time, he would have turned away from the sight of such poignant emotion.

He signaled to the Sikh. "Up the hill, Ram Singh! They're going to set off a demolition bomb! We've got to stop them!"

As they raced up, the Spider deftly inserted new clips in his automatics. Ram Singh did not need to reload his rifle, for the magazine was only half exhausted. He carried the gun in front of him, finger on the trigger.

"*Wallah!*" He shouted his tribal battle cry as he charged.

From the other side of the house, there came other sounds

of shouts and of shooting. The four bankers must have been admitted through the gate, with the hope of trapping them in the house, and they were coming up shooting, too.

The Spider, was slightly in the lead, and they were yet fifty feet from the house, when a small group of men came out on the run. In the lead was Bertram Flemming, carrying a submachine gun under his arm. Behind him were almost two dozen Indios, all armed, many carrying packs on their backs. The exodus had begun. *El Crocodilo* must have set his time bomb, and was making his escape by the back way.

Ram Singh had raised his rifle, but he held his fire on seeing Flemming. "It is the banker—"

"That's *El Crocodilo!*" the Spider shouted. He threw down his automatics and fired again and again. Flame and thunder belched from his muzzles, and in a split-second Ram Singh was also firing his rifle. Their barrage, delivered into the closely bunched group of Indios, did terrible damage. Half their number fell under the swift and deadly stream of slugs, and the others fled pell-mell.

El Crocodilo was wounded in the shoulder and the thigh, but he tried to crawl after his fleeing men.

The Spider reached his side in a flash, and kicked out of his hands the submachine gun which he had tried to train on him. He seized the wounded man by an arm, and slung him over his shoulder.

"Wait, wait!" cried Flemming, terrified at the sight of the Spider. "I'm wounded...."

"Sure!" said the Spider. "I'll get you to the house!"

"No, no! Not the house!" The Spider's laugh rang out harshly. He carried Flemming up the hill on the run, with Ram Singh at his side. Ram Singh showed his teeth in a gleaming smile. "Ah, pig! You do not thank the Spider for helping you!"

"Not to the house!" Flemming shrieked. "It's mined!"

"Too bad!" grated the Spider.

As they reached the house, they found Simmons and the other bankers standing around in bewilderment. They gaped when they saw Flemming slung across the Spider's shoulder.

"Gentlemen," the Spider told them, "meet *El Crocodilo.* No wonder all your plans were known!"

He dumped Flemming unceremoniously on the floor, while Ram Singh ran down the corridor looking for the prisoners. Nita's voice, shouting to him, drew him in the right direction, and in a moment he had her out. The two of them went from cell to cell, freeing the others.

Nita's color was high as she urged each of the freed hostages to leave the house.

"It's mined!" she told them. Then to Ram Singh, "I'm afraid it's too late anyway. *El Crocodilo* told me the mine would destroy everything within a thousand feet, and that it would go off five minutes after he left. Three minutes are gone!"

THEY ROUNDED the bend in the corridor, following the last of the freed prisoners, and saw the Spider, still carrying Flemming slung on his shoulder, go down a flight of stairs into the basement. Flemming was pointing frantically with his finger, and urging his captor to hurry.

"It's down in the cellar!" he shouted. "The mine switch. Hurry! Hurry!"

Nita stopped short, and Ram Singh too. They waited, breathless, while the Spider disappeared into the cellar.

"If the Spider dies down there," she said, "we—"

"We die with him, Mistress Nita!" Ram Singh boomed. "What is a better way to end life than in the company of one we love?"

From the doorway there came a sob.

Mrs. Delia Vandercook and Ellen had come up the hill, and had heard what Nita and Ram Singh had said.

"Get out, quickly!" Nita shouted. "The mine may go off—"

Mrs. Vandercook's eyes were shining, as her arms tightened about Ellen.

"We, too, prefer to await—the Spider!"

And so the four of them stood waiting for eternity to come upon them.

And then, they heard a step on the basement stairs, and the Spider reappeared, still carrying Flemming.

"You—you waited for me?"

Nita gulped, and nodded. "We—waited for you."

Slowly she came into his arms.

"Flemming stayed conscious long enough to show me the switch. I guess he prefers to live to stand trial."

He bent and kissed Nita softly on the lips.

"It's time for the Spider to leave," he said. "You, Ram Singh, can take care of turning Flemming over to the police." He turned and strode toward the door.

Mrs. Vandercook stopped him. She and Ellen looked up at him, and Ellen said, "I owe you my life, Spider! If I only knew who you were—"

"Shush, Ellen!" her mother rebuked her. "No one knows who the Spider is."

"No one?" the Spider asked.

"No one!" she said firmly. "I—I knew, but I—have forgotten. I only know that the Spider gave me back my little girl. I shall pray for him every night!"

"I, too!" said Ellen. With her hands still shackled behind her back, she came and stood on tiptoe and raised her face to his. He bent and kissed her forehead.

Then he walked out into the night.

POPULAR HERO PULPS  AVAILABLE NOW:

THE SPIDER

❑ #1: The Spider Strikes	$13.95
❑ #2: The Wheel of Death	$13.95
❑ #3: Wings of the Black Death	$13.95
❑ #4: City of Flaming Shadows	$13.95
❑ #5: Empire of Doom!	$13.95
❑ #6: Citadel of Hell	$13.95
❑ #7: The Serpent of Destruction	$13.95
❑ #8: The Mad Horde	$13.95
❑ #9: Satan's Death Blast	$13.95
❑ #10: The Corpse Cargo	$13.95
❑ #11: Prince of the Red Looters	$13.95
❑ #12: Reign of the Silver Terror	$13.95
❑ #13: Builders of the Dark Empire	$13.95
❑ #14: Death's Crimson Juggernaut	$13.95
❑ #15: The Red Death Rain	$13.95
❑ #16: The City Destroyer	$13.95
❑ #17: The Pain Emperor	$13.95
❑ #18: The Flame Master	$13.95
❑ #19: Slaves of the Crime Master	$13.95
❑ #20: Reign of the Death Fiddler	$13.95
❑ #21: Hordes of the Red Butcher	$13.95
❑ #22: Dragon Lord of the Underworld	$13.95
❑ #23: Master of the Death-Madness	$13.95
❑ #24: King of the Red Killers	$13.95
❑ #25: Overlord of the Damned	$13.95
❑ #26: Death Reign of the Vampire King	$13.95
❑ #27: Emperor of the Yellow Death	$13.95
❑ #28: The Mayor of Hell	$13.95
❑ #29: Slaves of the Murder Syndicate	$13.95
❑ #30: Green Globes of Death	$13.95
❑ #31: The Cholera King	$13.95
❑ #32: Slaves of the Dragon	$13.95
❑ #33: Legions of Madness	$12.95
❑ #34: Laboratory of the Damned	$12.95
❑ #35: Satan's Sightless Legion	$12.95
❑ #36: The Coming of the Terror	$12.95
❑ #37: The Devil's Death-Dwarfs	$12.95
❑ #38: City of Dreadful Night	$12.95
❑ #39: Reign of the Snake Men	$12.95
❑ #40: Dictator of the Damned	$12.95
❑ #41: The Mill-Town Massacres	$12.95
❑ #42: Satan's Workshop	$12.95
❑ #43: Scourge of the Yellow Fangs	$12.95
❑ #44: The Devil's Pawnbroker	$12.95
❑ #45: Voyage of the Coffin Ship	$12.95
❑ #46: The Man Who Ruled in Hell	$13.95
❑ #47: Slaves of the Black Monarch	$13.95
❑ #48: Machineguns Over the White House	$13.95
❑ #49: The City That Dared Not Eat	$13.95
❑ #50: Master of the Flaming Horde	$13.95
❑ #51: Satan's Switchboard	$13.95
❑ #52: Legions of the Accursed Light	$13.95
❑ #53: The City of Lost Men	$13.95
❑ #54: The Grey Horde Creeps	$13.95
❑ #55: City of Whispering Death	$13.95
❑ #56: When Thousands Slept in Hell	$13.95
❑ #57: Satan's Shakles	$14.95
❑ #58: The Emperor From Hell	$14.95
❑ #59: The Devil's Candlesticks	$14.95
❑ #60: The City That Paid to Die	$14.95
❑ #61: The Spider at Bay	$14.95
❑ #62: Scourge of the Black Legions	$14.95
❑ #63: The Withering Death	$14.95
❑ #64: Claws of the Golden Dragon	$14.95
❑ #65: The Song of Death	$14.95
❑ #66: The Silver Death Reign	$14.95
❑ #67: Blight of the Blazing Eye	$14.95
❑ #68: King of the Fleshless Legion	$14.95
❑ #69: Rule of the Monster Men	$16.95
❑ #70: The Spider and the Slaves of Hell	$16.95
❑ #71: The Spider and the Fire God	$16.95
❑ #72: The Corpse Broker	$16.95
❑ #73: The Spider and the Eyeless Legion	$16.95
❑ #74: The Spider and the Faceless One	$16.95
❑ #75: Satan's Murder Machines	$16.95
❑ #76: The Spider and the Pain Master	$16.95
❑ #77: Hell's Sales Manager	$16.95
❑ #78: Slaves of the Laughing Death	$16.95
❑ #79: The Man From Hell	$16.95
❑ #80: The Spider and the War Emperor	$16.95
❑ #81: Judgement of the Damned	$17.95
❑ ***NEW:*** #82: Dictator's Death-Merchants	$17.95

THE WESTERN RAIDER

❑ #1: Guns of the Damned	$13.95
❑ #2: The Hawk Rides Back from Death	$13.95
❑ #3: Gun-Call for the Lost Legion	$13.95
❑ #4: The Law of Silver Trent	$13.95
❑ #5: The Gun-Prayer of Silver Trent	$13.95
❑ #6: Silver Trent Rides Alone	$13.95

CAPTAIN SATAN

❑ #1: The Mask of the Damned	$13.95
❑ #2: Parole for the Dead	$13.95
❑ #3: The Dead Man Express	$13.95
❑ #4: A Ghost Rides the Dawn	$13.95
❑ #5: The Ambassador From Hell	$13.95

DR. YEN SIN

❑ #1: Mystery of the Dragon's Shadow	$12.95
❑ #2: Mystery of the Golden Skull	$12.95
❑ #3: Mystery of the Singing Mummies	$12.95

THE MASKED MARKSMAN

❑ #1: Death Takes an Encore	$16.95
❑ #2: Death's Understudy	$16.95
❑ #3: Death Steals the Act	$16.95
❑ #4: Top Billing for Murder	$16.95
❑ ***NEW:*** #5: Curtain Call for the Corpse	$17.95

POPULAR HERO PULPS  AVAILABLE NOW:

OPERATOR 5

- ❑ #1: The Masked Invasion $13.95
- ❑ #2: The Invisible Empire $13.95
- ❑ #3: The Yellow Scourge $13.95
- ❑ #4: The Melting Death $13.95
- ❑ #5: Cavern of the Damned $13.95
- ❑ #6: Master of Broken Men $13.95
- ❑ #7: Invasion of the Dark Legions $13.95
- ❑ #8: The Green Death Mists $13.95
- ❑ #9: Legions of Starvation $13.95
- ❑ #10: The Red Invader $13.95
- ❑ #11: The League of War-Monsters $13.95
- ❑ #12: The Army of the Dead $13.95
- ❑ #13: March of the Flame Marauders $13.95
- ❑ #14: Blood Reign of the Dictator $13.95
- ❑ #15: Invasion of the Yellow Warlords $13.95
- ❑ #16: Legions of the Death Master $13.95
- ❑ #17: Hosts of the Flaming Death $13.95
- ❑ #18: Invasion of the Crimson Death Cult $13.95
- ❑ #19: Attack of the Blizzard Men $13.95
- ❑ #20: Scourge of the Invisible Death $13.95
- ❑ #21: Raiders of the Red Death $13.95
- ❑ #22: War-Dogs of the Green Destroyer $13.95
- ❑ #23: Rockets From Hell $13.95
- ❑ #24: War-Masters from the Orient $13.95
- ❑ #25: Crime's Reign of Terror $13.95
- ❑ #26: Death's Ragged Army $13.95
- ❑ #27: Patriots' Death Battalion $13.95
- ❑ #28: The Bloody Forty-five Days $13.95
- ❑ #29: America's Plague Battalions $13.95
- ❑ #30: Liberty's Suicide Legions $13.95
- ❑ #31: Siege of the Thousand Patriots $13.95
- ❑ #32: Patriots' Death March $14.95
- ❑ #33: Revolt of the Lost Legions $14.95
- ❑ #34: Drums of Destruction $14.95
- ❑ #35: The Army Without a Country $14.95
- ❑ #36: The Bloody Frontiers $14.95
- ❑ #37: The Coming of the Mongol Hordes $14.95
- ❑ #38: The Siege That Brought Black Death $16.95
- ❑ #39: Revolt of the Devil Men $16.95
- ❑ #40: The Suicide Battalion $16.95
- ❑ #41: The Day of the Damned $16.95
- ❑ #42: The Dawn That Shook the World $16.95
- ❑ #43: When Hell Came to America $16.95
- ❑ #44: Invasion From the Sky $16.95
- ❑ #45: The Winged Horror of the Yellow Vulture $17.95

G-8 AND HIS BATTLE ACES

- ❑ #1: The Bat Staffel $13.95

CAPTAIN COMBAT

- ❑ #1: The Sky Beast of Berlin $13.95
- ❑ #2: Red Wings For the Blood Battalion $13.95
- ❑ #3: Low Ceiling For Nazi Hell Hawks $13.95

ACE G-MAN

- ❑ #1: The Suicide Squad Reports for Death $14.95
- ❑ #2: Coffins for the Suicide Squad $14.95
- ❑ #3: Shells for the Suicide Squad $14.95
- ❑ #4: The Suicide Squad in Corpse-Town $14.95
- ❑ #5: Wanted–In Three Pine Coffins $14.95
- ❑ #6: The Suicide Squad's Dawn Patrol $14.95
- ❑ #7: Targets for the Flaming Arrow $16.95

DUSTY AYRES AND HIS BATTLE BIRDS

- ❑ #1: Black Lightning! $13.95
- ❑ #2: Crimson Doom $13.95
- ❑ #3: The Purple Tornado $13.95
- ❑ #4: The Screaming Eye $13.95
- ❑ #5: The Green Thunderbolt $13.95
- ❑ #6: The Red Destroyer $13.95
- ❑ #7: The White Death $13.95
- ❑ #8: The Black Avenger $13.95
- ❑ #9: The Silver Typhoon $13.95
- ❑ #10: The Troposphere F-S $13.95
- ❑ #11: The Blue Cyclone $13.95
- ❑ #12: The Tesla Raiders $13.95

MAVERICKS

- ❑ #1: Five Against the Law $12.95
- ❑ #2: Mesquite Manhunters $12.95
- ❑ #3: Bait for the Lobo Pack $12.95
- ❑ #4: Doc Grimson's Outlaw Posse $12.95
- ❑ #5: Charlie Parr's Gunsmoke Cure $12.95

THE MYSTERIOUS WU FANG

- ❑ #1: The Case of the Six Coffins $12.95
- ❑ #2: The Case of the Scarlet Feather $12.95
- ❑ #3: The Case of the Yellow Mask $12.95
- ❑ #4: The Case of the Suicide Tomb $12.95
- ❑ #5: The Case of the Green Death $12.95
- ❑ #6: The Case of the Black Lotus $12.95
- ❑ #7: The Case of the Hidden Scourge $12.95

THE SECRET 6

- ❑ #1: The Red Shadow $13.95
- ❑ #2: House of Walking Corpses $13.95
- ❑ #3: The Monster Murders $13.95
- ❑ #4: The Golden Alligator $13.95

CAPTAIN ZERO

- ❑ #1: City of Deadly Sleep $13.95
- ❑ #2: The Mark of Zero! $13.95
- ❑ #3: The Golden Murder Syndicate $13.95

RED FINGER

- ❑ #1: Second-Hand Death $24.95

www.ingramcontent.com/pod-product-compliance
Lightning Source LLC
LaVergne TN
LVHW020628100826
845148LV00012B/2101

9781618278975